Dangerous Magic

Dangerous Magic

Jayne Ann Krentz
writing as Stephanie James

THORNDIKE
CHIVERS

This Large Print edition is published by Thorndike Press®, Waterville, Maine USA and by BBC Audiobooks, Ltd, Bath, England.

Published in 2005 in the U.S. by arrangement with Harlequin Books S.A.

Published in 2005 in the U.K. by arrangement with Harlequin Enterprises II B.V.

U.S. Hardcover 0-7862-6746-1 (Famous Authors)
U.K. Hardcover 1-4056-3274-7 (Chivers Large Print)
U.K. Softcover 1-4056-3275-5 (Camden Large Print)

The text of this Large Print edition is unabridged. Other aspects of the book may vary from the original edition.

Set in 16 pt. Plantin by Christina S. Huff.

Printed in the United States on permanent paper.

British Library Cataloguing-in-Publication Data available

Library of Congress Cataloging-in-Publication Data

James, Stephanie.
    Dangerous magic / Jayne Ann Krentz writing as Stephanie James.
        p. cm.
    ISBN 0-7862-6746-1 (lg. print : hc : alk. paper)
    1. Businesswomen — Fiction. 2. Large type books.
I. Title.
PS3561.R44D364 2004
813´.6—dc22   2004051710

Dangerous Magic

Chapter 1

Elissa Sheldon sat stunned, letting the full force of the insult wash over her in an icy wave. The only thing which kept her from drowning under the impact, she realized dimly, was the internal rage which rose to meet it. But that, too, was a problem because it took all her not inconsiderable will to master the fury before it mastered her.

"Would you," she said quite clearly, her low, slightly husky voice sounding incredibly restrained to her own ears, "mind repeating that?"

Her blue-green eyes, normally so alive with humor and a contagious enthusiasm for life, darkened rapidly to green flames, but the effect was lost on the tall, hard man standing at the window behind his desk. He had his back to her, apparently absorbed in watching the Seattle business-day traffic fifteen floors below.

"You heard me, Miss Sheldon," Wade Taggert growled softly. "I merely pointed out that you picked the wrong man to sleep with in your efforts to secure the promotion to head the editing and graphics department." He paused significantly. "You should have tried your wiles on me. Not Martin Randolph."

For an instant longer Elissa simply stared, appalled, at the lean, powerful masculine back across from her. Wade Taggert was dressed all wrong, she thought as a finger of near hysteria touched her mind. He ought to have been wearing skins and carrying a spear instead of being attired in a conservative dark suit, white shirt, and tie. But perhaps such clothing was *de rigueur* for the modern-day predator.

"Mr. Taggert," Elissa began a little desperately, all thought of the promotion disappearing in the face of the potential ramifications of his outrageous insult, "there is some mistake! I don't know where you got the idea that I would . . . would lower myself to that sort of behaviour, but you're wrong! I suppose you're one of those men who assume any woman anxious to get ahead in the business world will do anything to climb her way up the ladder, but I can assure you that you owe me an apology in this case!"

But even if he got down on his knees and apologized, Elissa realized as she tried to contain her anger, there was no way in the world she could continue to work for this man. His accusation would always be the dominant factor between them, making any sort of business relationship impossible.

"I saw the necklace, Elissa." The deep, heavy-timbred voice was curiously devoid of intonation, almost weary-sounding, as Wade Taggert turned around at last.

Elissa met the shock of his icy gray eyes and wanted to turn and flee. Only her fierce pride and grim determination to set him straight kept her in the chair. Facing Taggert was a formidable task at any time, but when he was in this remote and glacial mood, all normally intimidating features were magnified.

He was thirty-five years old, and none of those thirty-five years looked to have been easy. He had recently been appointed manager of the Seattle office of the computer-design firm for which Elissa worked, and the office grapevine rumored him to be in line for the chief executive officer position of the company. Elissa didn't doubt it. Wade Taggert had made his way rapidly and ruthlessly up through the ranks in a relatively short time, and there was no reason to think he wouldn't keep going. He had done a lot for CompuDesign, and the company would undoubtedly keep rewarding him.

The image of a predator hardened in Elissa's mind as she absorbed the sight of him outlined against the city skyline. Taggert's near-black hair was cut in an unfashionably severe line, revealing wings of gray at each temple. Heavy brows framed deep-set eyes which ranged from the present wintry gray to a strange silvery color, depending, Elissa supposed, on the light. The planes of his face had been chiseled with an iron hand, leaving the tanned skin stretched tautly over the commanding cheekbones and a square, aggressive chin. Fine lines fanned out from the corners of his eyes, making it appear as if he had spent a fair amount of time outdoors. There were harsh grooves etched at the sides of his stern mouth. And, as was the case with most efficient predators, there wasn't an ounce of extra weight on the man. Broad shoulders and chest tapered to lean waist and hips which were emphasized by the close, conservative cut of his clothes.

Elissa felt his gaze raking her as she sat tensely in the chair, and she realized he was taking in the neat tailored green suit along with the short, sassy style of her dark auburn hair, which was cut into the nape and made a perfect frame for the slightly slanting sea-colored eyes. There was no great beauty to be discovered in the face, she knew, although her small, firm chin, faintly tip-tilted nose, and well-drawn cheekbones went together in a reasonably attractive fashion. It was the expressiveness of those features and the overall impression of laughter and challenge which drew the occasional second glance. Her five feet four inches of slender height put her at a disadvantage, she felt, compared to her accuser's six feet of coordinated strength. But her clothes were expensive and fit the small, gentle curves of her breast and hip well without being overpowering.

Very coolly, Elissa crossed her legs in a small gesture of feminine challenge. She was twenty-seven years old, and she hadn't gotten this far without having learned something about staying calm under fire. She would not let this man see how badly affected she was by the unexpected and shattering scene.

"What necklace, Mr. Taggert?" she demanded, lifting her chin and narrowing the blue-green eyes a bit further to let him know she didn't appreciate his use of her first name.

"The one Randolph gave you the other

night, presumably for services rendered. Too bad he didn't have the power to repay you in full, but you should have verified that before getting involved with that sort of bargain. If it makes you feel any better, he did put your name in for consideration," Taggert drawled bitingly.

"But you, in your infinite wisdom, disregarded the recommendation?" Elissa concluded evenly, unaware that the knuckles of the hand clenched in her lap had gone quite white under the force she was exert- ing.

"You were very well qualified, being the supervisor of the technical writing department," he admitted.

"But I, er, bestowed my favors on the wrong man?" she gritted.

"I'm surprised at you, Elissa," he told her bleakly. "You should have done your homework better."

"Could we get back to the little matter of the necklace? It appears to be the chief item of evidence."

"What about it?" He shrugged, turning slightly away and prowling across the room to sample the view from the side window. The advantages of a corner office, Elissa thought with a sigh. She knew what he was seeing from that vantage point; the busy harbor and Elliott Bay with its myriad white ferries gliding to and from the various islands. The Seattle winter day was as cold and gray as the atmosphere in the office.

"I only want to know where and when you saw me receiving the thing."

"After work the other night, down in the garage. You were standing with Randolph beside his car. I saw him take it out of the box and hand it to you."

"And on that basis you denied me a promotion and accused me of sleeping my way up the corporate ladder?" Elissa blazed.

He swung around and trapped her flaming gaze. "It's not the first time I've seen you under less than innocent circumstances with Martin Randolph. You were out with him the other night in the cocktail lounge in the lobby of the hotel down the street. He's a married man, Elissa, and you know it."

"If you know that, then you should know the necklace was a present he'd bought for his wife. I was merely admiring it," she shot back, still trying desperately to keep her temper from exploding completely.

"You put it into your purse," he retorted grimly. "Don't lie to me, Elissa. It won't work."

"I'm keeping it for June Randolph's surprise birthday party, which happens to be tomorrow night. At my apartment, I might add! June and I are good friends."

"Then you shouldn't be having after-work drinks with her husband, should you?" Taggert snapped.

"Just how many such occasions have you witnessed, Mr. Taggert?" Elissa got out between painfully dry lips.

"Enough," he muttered laconically, walking back to his desk and dropping into the chair behind it. "Two or three, at least."

"And you're not in the least prepared to believe they might have been totally innocent events, are you?"

"It's a bit too convenient, Elissa. You didn't start meeting Randolph after hours until the time for this promotion drew close —"

"As close as June's surprise party! That's all that was being planned during those incriminating little meetings!"

"Don't try to play me for a fool," he ordered, leaning back in the large chair and eyeing her harshly. "On at least one occasion I saw you take the elevator upstairs. Randolph followed a few minutes later."

"I hope you enjoyed yourself playing I Spy," Elissa hissed, unable to believe what was happening. "If you knew that hotel well, you'd know the rest rooms are on the second level where the convention facilities are located. Good grief! What did you do? Hide behind the potted palms and conduct surveillance operations on your employees? Perhaps you should try working for the government!"

"I had to be sure," he stated flatly, ignoring her sarcasm. There was something very heavy and final in his dark voice. Elissa shivered involuntarily.

"And now you are sure?" she demanded, startled at the degree of her own anger. Never had she been so infuriated. She glared at her tormentor, her mind whirling with alternative courses of action.

"I think the evidence of my own eyes is fairly conclusive, Elissa," Wade Taggert said coldly. "There's really not much point in going through it again, is there? Why don't you just accept the fact that I found out what was going on and that your methods worked against you?"

"And Evelyn Keenan got the job, even though she's had less experience and has been with the company for a shorter time," Elissa stated.

"Are you going to accuse her of having slept with the right man?" he asked, one heavy brow lifting quizzically.

"Don't be ridiculous," she snapped back in utter scorn. "Evelyn would never do such a thing!" Which was nothing less than the truth, Elissa thought moodily. Pretty, blond, hazel-eyed, and quite competent, Evelyn was also very much in love with her new husband.

"I must admit you're being fair about the matter, at any rate," Wade retorted. "You're right. Evelyn got the job because she was the second-most-qualified person around."

"The *most* qualified person having foolishly put herself out of the running by choosing the wrong man to seduce?" Elissa could almost feel the blood simmering in her veins now. Somehow she would find a way to take this man down a peg or two if it was the last thing she did on earth! "Tell me something, Mr. Taggert, did you put pressure on Evelyn to sleep with you and then have to give her the job anyway when she wouldn't?"

"No!" he flung back, sounding genuinely outraged himself. "Unlike you, I choose my bedmates from the unmarried crowd!"

Elissa felt the wave of red storming into her cheeks, and it became all she could do to maintain eye contact with that bitter gray gaze. In spite of the knowledge of her own innocence of the charges the man had leveled against her, it was difficult to meet the power in him on an even footing. My God! she thought wonderingly. If I had been guilty, I would have been crawling out the door on my hands and knees by now!

"I see," she managed gamely. "Then why didn't you simply come to me and tell me what the conditions for getting the job were?"

"Because," he grated softly, significantly, "I wanted to teach you a lesson."

"A lesson in how to choose the right man next time?" she rasped furiously.

"Something like that," he acknowledged sardonically. In an absent gesture, Wade reached out and picked up a yellow pencil lying near his hand. He tapped it gently on the blotter while he assessed her bitter gaze. "If you're going to use such techniques to rise to the top of the heap, Elissa, you might as well practice them on me. I'm in a much better position to assist your career efforts than Randolph, and I hope this little matter of the promotion proves it."

"You," she gritted between fiercely clenched teeth, her slender body almost shaking now with the force of her emotions, "are the most unprincipled, egotistical, ruthless man I have ever had the misfortune to meet!"

"I think we understand each other perfectly," he shot back dryly.

How could he sit there as if he were lord of all he surveyed? Elissa asked herself almost frantically. There was such absolute masculine certainty on that hard face, such undisguised, aggression in those gray eyes. Wade Taggert was, indeed, a predator, and she had been elected the prey!

"There's not much point in carrying this conversation any further, is there?" she finally asked bleakly, shaking her head once in a gesture of disbelief. This couldn't be happening! "I'll let you have my resignation as soon as I can get back to my desk." She moved her trembling fingers to the arms of her chair in preparation for rising, but his next words brought her head up with a snap, the short auburn hair dancing gracefully about her small ears.

"I'm not asking for your resignation, Elissa. I'm merely pointing out the facts of life to you. Your work for CompuDesign has been excellent in the month and a half that I've headed this office. The records show it's been excellent for the four years you've worked for the firm. You had no need to resort to the methods you used in trying to land this latest promotion, but if you are going to use such methods . . . ."

The pencil in his fingers snapped as the sentence was allowed to trail off meaningfully.

"If I am going to use such methods I might as well learn to use them where they'll do the most good, is that it?" she heard herself say.

"As I said," he repeated in a voice of sandpaper on silk, "I think we understand each other very well."

"There's a term for what you're doing to me," she breathed tightly, still keeping her seat in the chair but feeling as if she would leap to her feet and run like any other small creature if the hunter made a sudden move toward her. "It's called sexual harassment, and it's illegal!"

"There's a term for women who use their bodies to get what they want on the job," he snarled, spreading his palms flat on the top of the hardwood desk and holding her pinned beneath his contemptuous gaze. "Several terms, in fact. None of them particularly flattering!"

"If you think so little of me, I'm surprised you're even bothering to issue a proposition," Elissa bit out. The first faint glimmerings of an idea were beginning to shape themselves in her much-pressed brain. This man was so certain he had everything figured out. What would it do to his ego to discover he was wrong?

"Men, to their eternal bewilderment, cannot always account for their own tastes, Elissa," Wade Taggert told her with something approaching wry humor in his words. "I want you. It's as simple as that, and I'm using the main lure I have to get you."

Elissa stared at him, uncomprehendingly. "Want me," she repeated dully, her blue-green eyes blinking once as if to clear away a figment of her imagination. But he was still there, sitting behind the wide desk with all the cool, waiting patience of a large cat. The gray eyes were enigmatic pools of cold, icy rain, and the grim line of his mouth was made no less harsh by the curious little upward quirk at one corner. One hand continued to play with the broken piece of pencil in an idle fashion.

"You find that so difficult to understand?" he asked almost mildly. "In the short time I've been here I haven't noticed you suffering from a shortage of admirers."

"They're called friends, Mr. Taggert," Elissa snapped, goaded. And it was true, she thought somewhat vaguely. She did have a lot of friends, and certainly some of them were male; but the one man who fit the description of admirer didn't even work for

CompuDesign! Wade Taggert couldn't have been further off base then to think of her as a *femme fatale!*

"And what do you call Martin Randolph?" he prodded bluntly.

"I call him a friend who happens to be fifteen years older than I am *and* happily married as I told you before!"

"Which puts him out of the risk category, doesn't it? You can use him on the assumption that he isn't in a position to demand anything more than you feel like giving. But what happens if he goes crazy, as other men have been known to do, and leaves his wife for you? What will you do if he comes knocking at your door some night expecting to be taken in by the woman who's been showing him so much attention? Will you feel even a little guilty, Elissa?" Taggert was suddenly surging to his feet, but he made no move toward her. Instead he turned back to the window behind his desk, and she was once again left with his broad back as a target.

"That's hardly likely to happen!"

"I agree," he said surprisingly, glancing back at her over his shoulder. "Because I've put a stop to your little game with him by removing the prize and giving it to someone else. Randolph's no fool. He'll soon realize

21

you're pursuing more promising avenues of advancement, and if he's smart he'll thank his lucky stars he got out of the situation before he did something really stupid like leaving his wife!" He shifted completely back around to face her, planting his large hands flat on his desk and leaning forward with cool challenge in every line of his body. "Well, Elissa?" He waited.

Elissa pulled her scrambling thoughts into some order, trying to come up with a way to handle the incredible situation. Only one thing seemed very clear in the chaos, and that was that if there was any way of achieving even a token revenge against this man, she was going to take it.

"Well, what?" she taunted bravely. "You can't expect me to leap at your offer when I still don't know why you've made it." She was stalling for time now as her earlier idea took firmer shape. "You might think I was dumb enough to sleep with the wrong man once for business purposes, but don't make the mistake of thinking I'll make the same error again!" There was no point arguing her own case any longer. Elissa accepted that with bitter resolve. She would devote all her energy now to finding another tactic to use against Wade Taggert. A tactic that would show him once and for all he had no right to play havoc with the careers of the women who worked for him. A tactic that would demonstrate his own fallibility . . .

"I've told you why I'm inviting you to investigate other possibilities for career advancement," he drawled. "I want you. I don't know how long I'll want you," he added ruthlessly, "but while I do, you might be able to benefit considerably. I'm sure your imagination can supply you with all the potential inherent in the situation. You couldn't aim any higher than the division office manager, could you, Elissa? Unless, of course, you tried for the CEO! But perhaps, if you play your cards right and keep me interested long enough, you'll find yourself moving up right along with me."

Elissa whitened. Never in her life had she been subjected to such unsubtle propositioning! "I see your own career path is on course, Mr. Taggert. There's no doubt in your own mind that you'll be the next CEO? The next chief executive officer of CompuDesign?" she demanded gratingly, trying to achieve a semblance of cool contempt.

"If I want it badly enough," he told her starkly, "I'll get it." Quite suddenly Elissa believed him. If this man really went after a goal, he fully expected to get it.

"It doesn't make any sense," she murmured after a second's tense silence. "Why me? There are far more beautiful women working for you, Mr. Taggert, and you're not blind. Several of them are even unmarried!" she concluded mockingly.

"I agree you're not the most beautiful or sophisticated woman I've ever met, Elissa Sheldon," he told her, his mouth twisting slightly. "But there is something about you which attracts me. For the time being, at any rate," he added with casual menace.

He circled the desk then, moving so quickly that Elissa was only half out of her chair and nowhere near en route for the door by the time he reached her. In two long pantherlike strides he was in front of her, reaching down to pull her up out of her seat. His hands clamped around her arms, and she was held immobile as he brought her very close to him.

"For a while," he went on in a voice of distant, grating thunder, "I want to know what it's like to be included in the warmth of your smile. I want to answer the challenge in your eyes, and I want to join with you in the laughter. I want to argue about the stock market and about politics, and I want to enjoy your enthusiasm, for life. In short, Elissa, I want to be part of your charmed circle. But there's one stipulation: While I'm circling in your obit, I will be the *only* one there. Is that understood?"

"Let me go!" Elissa cried in astonishment and a hint of genuine fear. "Take your hands off me this instant!" Her fingers splayed against the dark material of his jacket as she faced him, wide-eyed and wary. Desperately she pushed, trying to put distance between them, but he didn't appear to notice.

"I asked if you understood my basic requirement for this affair of ours," he countered roughly, giving her a small shake.

"I heard what you said, damn it!" she flung back, stung. The look on his face and the unshakable strength in him warned her to tread carefully until she was once again free of his grasp. "But we have no affair, so your 'requirements' don't matter a whole lot, do they?" That had been unwise, but Elissa was too angry to still her tongue.

"We will be having one," he swore softly, "when you've had a chance to simmer down and think about what I can do for you. And I'll throw in something else for your consideration," he went on, tightening his grasp until she was pressed unwillingly against the length of his tough, hard frame.

"What's that?" she taunted bitterly. "A

diamond necklace? It *was* diamond, you know, the one Martin gave me the other evening —"

"This is what I had in mind," he interrupted harshly and lowered his head in a swift, unexpected move that caught her vulnerable mouth unprepared.

Elissa's small sound of outrage was totally muffled by the impact of Wade's kiss. It was a marauding, claiming, branding thing that promised fire and male dominance in no uncertain terms. Without any subtlety he forced apart her lips, his tongue sweeping boldly into the dark warmth of her mouth. It was a short, punishing foray designed only to demonstrate her inferior strength, and it succeeded in leaving her trembling with dismay and fury.

Hating her own helplessness in his arms, Elissa tried the only defense left to her and deliberately went passive in his ironclad embrace.

"That's better," he approved huskily as he sensed her lack of struggle. "Things will go much more smoothly if you don't fight me." His mouth continued to move over hers, seeking out the corners. When she would have turned her head aside, his teeth somehow caught her tender lower lip and closed on it with insolent, gentle promise.

She stood very still, letting the force of his chastising passion spend itself, her eyes shut against the reality of what was happening. Later, she vowed silently, later she would teach this arrogant man a lesson he would never forget!

She felt his hands move at last, releasing their grip on her arms and sliding around her waist. Elissa waited tensely, hoping for an opportunity to free herself, but even as she weighed the odds, she was being arched into the hard line of his thighs and her throat was becoming the focus of his determined mouth. She was aware of the intent in him in the most elemental way a woman can become aware of a man, and the knowledge was an added danger Elissa recognized only belatedly. It was only when the fundamental electricity in him began transferring itself to her through the contact points of hands and thigh and lips that she faced a new kind of fear.

"No!" she breathed grimly, refusing to allow her new inner despair to show in her voice. "I won't allow you to do this to me!" Could he know, she wondered desperately, just *what* he was beginning to do to her? How could her body react so traitorously to a man who promised nothing but insults and punishment! But it was beginning to react, and she had to stop the assault before her knees gave way completely.

"Why don't you allow me to kiss you, Elissa?" he mocked, dropping tiny, stinging caresses along her jaw and at the edge of her mouth. "Think of all I can do for you in exchange. And there's no wife waiting in the background to make matters difficult this time," he went on coaxingly. "You'll have entire nights to practice your magic on me. Who knows how far you can go in this company?"

With all her self-control, Elissa stifled the temptation to hurl all the verbal abuse she could think of back at him. At this dangerous juncture she must keep her priorities straight, and the most important thing was to get free of him. The second most vital matter was to set the stage for revenge, no matter how puny it might turn out to be. She would not let Wade Taggert treat her like this and get off scot-free!

"I'm listening to you," she muttered bitterly. "There's not much else I can do until you stop playing out your little scene. But you have to admit I've got some readjusting to do. I hardly expected this when you summoned me to the office this afternoon."

He lifted his head at that remark, leaving one last rather fierce kiss on her mouth before he did so. The gray eyes gazed brood-ingly down at her upturned face, and she could see the deliberation in them. He was wondering if she'd begun to see matters his way.

"You expected to be told you'd gotten the promotion, didn't you?" he demanded mus-ingly.

"It was a logical assumption on my part," she retorted, aware of the bruised feeling of her mouth. His embrace had been more in the nature of an attack, she thought fleet-ingly. As if Wade Taggert wanted it clear from the outset that he would be calling the shots between them.

"There will be other promotions, other possibilities," he told her with cool promise. His hands were still around her waist, and she could feel the strength in his fingers as they almost absently kneaded the lower curve of her back. It was a startlingly erotic sensation, she discovered to her horror, and one he wasn't even going out of his way to perform.

"Will there?" she questioned carefully, moving slightly and finding herself able to put a couple of inches between their bodies. She waited breathlessly for the next oppor-tunity to push for her freedom. Deliberately she kept her wide, sea-colored eyes on his face, trying to project the uncertainty of a woman seriously considering exchanging lovers. She would allow him to think he was winning the cruel game. It was the surest way to free herself for the moment. The future could take care of itself.

"Give me what I want, little witch," he whispered hoarsely, searching her face intently, "and you have my word I'll take care of you. Your time spent amusing me will pay dividends."

"And what you want is me?" she verified one last time, a small part of her still not entirely able to believe the shock which had occurred in his office this afternoon. "For some unspecified length of time?"

"Yes!" he grated thickly, and the fingers along her back dug into her flesh with controlled violence, as if he would take her then and there had he seen any way to manage it.

Elissa winced at his touch and what it implied. "Have you always satisfied your male urges in this manner? Using your position to tempt the woman you want?" It was difficult to keep the scorn out of her voice, but she strove for neutrality. He mustn't suspect she was forming plans of her own.

"Different women are tempted by different things," he retorted unhelpfully. "I've never tried quite this approach before, however." He smiled with a touch of cruelty. "But, then, I've never encountered one quite so determined to advance her career. Would you believe it? Most of them start thinking in terms of marriage rather than promotion."

Elissa flushed under his mockery. "You, of course, would never go that far to satisfy a temporary craving."

"Of course not," he agreed at once.

Elissa stepped back experimentally, and his hands dropped to his sides as he watched her move a few paces away and put the barrier of the chair between them. Clutching the edge of it with hands that might have shook otherwise, she faced him again, her head high.

"What guarantee do I have that you would keep your end of the bargain?" she challenged, working through the final steps of her poorly formed plan.

"Not much," he admitted freely, sweeping aside the edges of his jacket to plant his fists on his hips. He propped himself casually on the corner of the desk, legs stretched out straight in front of him, and watched her with lazy interest. She knew he sensed victory. Let him enjoy it, she told herself furiously. My time will come. "You really have only my word to rely on at this point," he concluded.

"And that's supposed to be enough?" she retorted.

"What more do you want?" he asked in some amusement.

"Perhaps a necklace . . ." she suggested baitingly.

"Necklaces, especially diamond necklaces, come after you've shown you can be trusted to keep your end of the deal," he murmured softly, the gray rain in his eyes washing over her face.

"You're asking me to trust you?"

"I'm less of a risk than Martin Randolph, and I have more to offer," he pointed out laconically.

She lifted one delicate brow but did not contradict him. "Aren't you afraid others will talk?" she asked instead.

"It's a big town," he growled. "We can get sufficiently lost in it after hours. There would, naturally, be no open signs of a — shall we call it an association? — between us at work. You wouldn't want people to say you were rising in the company because of me, would you? I think we can do a little better in the discretion department than you were doing with Randolph. We certainly won't see each other in the local lounges where the crowd hangs out after work." His sarcastic tone implied she wasn't well versed in the fine art of romantic intrigue.

Unconsciously Elissa tipped her pert head to one side and drummed the fingers of one hand against the back of the chair. "How soon," she murmured deliberately, "do you want an answer?"

"Is there any need for a delay?" he pounced immediately, his gray gaze slitting as he watched her.

"I, uh, think I deserve some time to consider the matter in more depth," she grated dryly. "A woman doesn't just plunge into these things without some thought."

"What more is there to consider? It all seems pretty obvious to me."

Elissa drew a deep breath and then jumped in with both feet. "Would you," she asked quietly, "wait until tomorrow night for your answer?"

There was a tense pause, and she was left with the conviction he had fully intended to seal the bargain that very night. Arrogant, pompous, egotistical male!

"Saturday night?" he repeated slowly, thoughtfully.

"Yes. Could you come by my place around seven? I'll have an answer ready by then," she promised, excitement threatening to swamp her at the boldness of her own plans. "Please, Wade?" she tacked on in as artfully pleading a style as she could manage under the circumstances.

It did the trick, however. With a curt nod of his head, Wade Taggert straightened, coming to his full six feet beside the desk. "Seven o'clock tomorrow evening, then. I'll be there," he vowed coolly, the male anticipation in him very evident. He was granting her the time, she realized abruptly, because he had no doubt about the outcome.

Biting her tongue to keep from screaming at him like a fishwife, Elissa grabbed her purse and fled with as much dignity as possible from the panther's cage.

Chapter 2

Of all the humiliating factors involved in the disastrous meeting on Friday afternoon, the one which kept returning to haunt Elissa all day Saturday was the look of triumph which had been in Wade Taggert's eyes when she'd left his office. Never had she seen that expression in the eyes of a male looking at her. The cold gray gaze had held an elemental masculine promise which appeared totally unhampered by the layers of civilization and sophistication that should have intervened.

It was only later in the day as she finished preparations for June Randolph's surprise party that Elissa realized her astonishment at her boss's behavior toward her had prompted her to overlook another, equally astounding matter: the way she had reacted to him and to his accusations.

Elissa paused halfway through icing the cake and stared unseeingly at the painting of a bizarre, other-worldly landscape hanging on the opposite kitchen wall. The painting didn't quite fit into the extraordinarily comfortable apartment furnishings, nor did it seem to go with the functional, neat kitchen. But, then, the five other strange, alien landscapes hanging throughout the one-bedroom high-rise apartment didn't seem to complement the overall decor, either. When visitors pointed that fact out, Elissa laughed, declared she was entitled to one idiosyncrasy, and motioned them to one of the very comfortable overstuffed chairs. Said visitors generally proceeded to prop their feet on the convenient hassock, settle back with the cup of tea or glass of wine which was always offered, and pour out their hearts on whatever subject happened to be uppermost in their minds at the time. And Elissa, in her instinctively enthusiastic, sympathetic fashion, gave her visitors, in addition to tea or wine, what it was they seemed to want most from a friend. Sometimes that involved an understanding ear, a gentle lecture, a crafty suggestion, or a good laugh.

Elissa gave such things automatically and easily, fully aware of what she was doing but not begrudging the gift. The rewards for such charm had come frequently and easily to her. They included good friends, good grades through college, relatives who had thought her enormously mature even as a young girl, and a good job.

Or at least, Elissa sighed grimly, returning her attention to the cake in front of her, a good job with steady advancement *had* been a part of the taken-for-granted things in her comfortable life-style until yesterday afternoon!

Her fingers wielded the icing knife with absent skill and she frowned down on her work as she considered the shock she had been put through on Friday. The greatest shock of all, naturally, was that anyone could have even conceived of her being guilty of the sort of behavior Wade Taggert had suggested. And if someone had been so crazy as to believe her capable of stooping to such unscrupulous actions, the incredible mistake should have been recognized as soon as Elissa declared her innocence. No one in his right mind could have believed Elissa Sheldon guilty of anything underhanded or degrading!

But how much did she really know about Wade Taggert? Elissa asked herself seriously as she stood back to admire her handiwork on the cake with a practiced eye. He'd only taken over the reins of CompuDesign a month and a half earlier. Perhaps he wasn't in his right mind, she told herself with a rueful attempt at humor. There had to be something a little crazy about a man who trailed his female employees to local cock-tail lounges after work!

She set the cake aside and began getting out the plates and napkins. Elissa entertained so frequently and so successfully that the work involved in a major production such as Jane's surprise party was almost second nature. The food would be elaborate and very good; the wine and other alcoholic beverages would be excellent. She would see to it that no one became embarrassingly or dangerously drunk, and everyone would have a great time. They always did.

But tonight, Elissa thought with a strange satisfaction as she artfully arranged the buffet table in front of the huge living-room window, there would be one exception to the rule. Wade Taggert was not going to enjoy himself in the least. And for very nearly the first time in her life since she was a small girl, Elissa found herself looking forward to another person's discomfort with a degree of enthusiasm that amazed her.

She wondered idly if having invited the boss would bother her friends, most of whom worked for CompuDesign. They would all be aware by now of the surprising fact that she hadn't gotten the promotion, although they couldn't know the humiliating reason why it had been denied. Elissa winced once again at the recollection of the Friday interview.

It wasn't just the fact that Taggert had denied her the advancement which would make people wonder why he was invited. It was also the fact that he was new and a complete change from the branch's former manager, a paternal gentleman who had retired. During his short time at the helm Wade Taggert had made it clear that he did not follow in the kindly footsteps of his predecessor. Nor did he go out of his way to fraternize with his employees as the older man had done.

Taggert was, Elissa decided as she showered an hour before the party, the perfect example of the lone wolf who had risen through the ranks on the basis of ability and ruthlessness. And wolf, she told herself as she toweled dry with one of the huge oversized bath sheets, was the operative word!

No, she would never have deliberately set out to make a friend of Wade Taggert, and he, in the normal course of events, would never have drifted into what he himself had termed Elissa's charmed circle. He was one of the rare individuals who would not have been welcomed there, nor could Elissa envision him as wanting to be a part of it.

But for tonight, she decided with grim anticipation, he would be invited into the comfortable, cheerful warmth which surrounded her. Because that was the most efficient technique she could use to prove to him how completely wrong he had been about her.

As she stood in front of the bedroom mirror, which was flanked by two of the strange landscapes featuring crumbling castles and grotesque creatures, Elissa wondered what sort of apology she would receive from the arrogant, so-certain-of-himself Wade Taggert. A curiously expectant little smile touched the corners of her generous, expressive mouth, and the blue-green eyes looked back at her from under long auburn lashes with an unfamiliar gleam. Taggert would find his disgusting challenge met with the full force of the truth, and she hoped his masculine pride would prod him into a suitably abject act of contrition.

Elissa spent the last few minutes before the party began thinking of various ways in which she could receive her boss's apology. She glanced at the hall clock as the doorbell rang. It was just six. With any luck, by the time Wade Taggert arrived at seven the party would be in full swing. She would time the cake so that he would be there when June discovered the lovely diamond necklace inside. And that, she decided vengefully, would be the *pièce de résistance!*

A last negligent glance in the hall mirror satisfied Elissa that she looked the proper hostess. Her long plaid wool skirt and lacy, old-fashioned blouse provided a warm, homey look that was at the same time fashionable. The sleek, sassy cap of dark red hair was brushed to a natural shine, and when she opened the door to her first guest, she knew her appearance was more than acceptable.

"Dean!" she exclaimed happily, flinging open the door to see the polished, handsome man standing outside in the hall. "You're the first to arrive! Come in, come in," she urged happily, putting a hand on Dean Norwood's expensively attired arm and standing on tiptoe for his light kiss. She smiled up at him as she led him inside, thinking, not for the first time, that this man, who was steadily becoming more and more important in her life, was a most attractive specimen. His light brown hair was cut and styled in a fashionable but not the least radical manner. The perfectly trimmed mustache added a touch of sophistication which was well carried out in the expensive tailoring of his designer suit, and Elissa knew the leather in his shoes was Italian. Dean's cheerful blue eyes smiled down at her as he followed her into the living room.

"And how was Wall Street this week?" she demanded, escorting him to a chair and moving over to the small bar to pour him his favorite drink. "I didn't catch the news last night, I'm afraid." Primarily, she added wryly to herself, because she'd been so upset after the meeting with Wade Taggert.

"The market closed down a bit, but not bad. The latest government figures on consumer spending affected it, of course, but things should be bouncing back on Monday," Dean told her pleasantly, reaching happily for the martini she was holding out to him. Elissa always mixed perfect martinis, just the way he liked them.

"The eternal optimism of the professional stockbroker," she teased, perching lightly on the wide arm of the overstuffed chair and tilting her head to smile down at him. "But I suppose when you're handling other people's money you have to keep them thinking there's hope around the corner."

"Can't have the clients panicking on me." Dean grinned, lounging back comfortably and reaching out to pat Elissa's knee with casual affection. "You're supposed to be the one with the big news tonight, though, love. Let's have it. I assume I am now drinking a salute to the new head of editing and graphics at CompuDesign?" He cocked a confident, querying eyebrow up at her.

Elissa grimaced and then attempted a rather rueful smile. "You are saluting the old and familiar supervisor of technical writing, Dean. My friend Evelyn Keenan got the promotion." Two seconds of inner debate was sufficient to convince Elissa not to go into details. She could think of no suitable way of telling her friend that she had been accused of trying to sleep her way to the top.

"Evelyn? The little blonde who got married a couple months ago?" Dean frowned in surprise. "But she's rather new, isn't she? She couldn't possibly have your experience."

"Taggert thought her perfectly qualified," Elissa said quietly. "And she is, Dean. I'm sure she'll do a fine job."

"But I was sure from what you'd told me that you had it in the bag."

"A good lesson in counting one's chickens before they're hatched," Elissa muttered, getting to her feet to answer the door as the bell sounded again.

"Elissa, you should have had that job!

What went wrong?" Dean's offended tones were balm to her spirit as she glanced at him over her shoulder.

"I'll tell you all about it later. Promise me you won't say anything to make Evelyn or her husband uncomfortable?"

"Of course not," he denied instantly. "But . . ."

"Later, Dean," she promised, her hand on the doorknob. "Although there's really nothing much to say about it."

The doorbell began to ring more and more frequently after that as the guests hurried to make the six-thirty deadline. Everyone wanted to be present when Martin Randolph escorted his wife into the room.

Over and over again Elissa listened to the same dismayed greeting as people bustled in from the wintry Seattle night. "Elissa! I heard about the promotion going to Evelyn. Thought sure you had it!"

And over and over again, Elissa summoned her most self-mocking smile, made jokes about counting chickens, and urged everyone to forget the matter with a shrug and the assuring words, "Evelyn will do a terrific job."

When Evelyn and her new husband arrived, there was something besides dismay in the younger woman's pretty hazel eyes.

There was a kind of nervous wariness which Elissa saw at once and set out to remove with automatic, efficient ease.

"Evelyn! Congratulations!" she beamed, holding open the door and urging the couple inside. "I know you're going to do a heck of a job. Taggert knew enough to recognize the quality work you did on that quarterly report last month, and I'm very glad for you." With a casual, congratulatory hug that set everyone who witnessed it at ease, the small tension passed as if it had never existed. No one ever stayed tense long at Elissa's parties.

The exception tonight, Elissa reminded herself with satisfaction, would be Wade Taggert, who, if he had an ounce of integrity in his large, hard frame, would be properly tense with the knowledge of his error. Or were wolves ever repentant? That thought occurred to her as she stood temporarily to one side, watching her guests relax and begin to enjoy themselves. She sipped idly at a glass of wine and considered the matter. Well, time would tell. It was six-thirty, time for June to walk in and be properly surprised. After that the real countdown would begin for Elissa. The turning point of her evening would be the instant she opened the door at seven o'clock and Wade Taggert absorbed the fact that her excuse about the surprise party had been valid.

The first highlight of the evening went off in a perfectly orchestrated fashion. Dark-haired and attractive, June Randolph entered the room on her equally dark-haired and attractive husband's arm. Both were in their forties, well-dressed, and clearly in love. The marriage was a second time around for each, and Elissa knew they were committed to making it a success.

The shouts of surprise and congratulations stormed over the apartment as June stood flushed with pleasure and excitement. Martin Randolph caught Elissa's eye over his wife's head and grinned conspiratorially.

"I told her we were just going to stop by for a drink." He chuckled, slipping off June's coat.

"Good heavens!" June gasped, laughing. "How long have you been planning this?"

"Almost a month." Martin smiled, vastly pleased with the success of what he had come to think of as his own idea. Somewhere in the excitement of planning the party the fact that Elissa had given him the notion had slipped his mind. She didn't mind. There was nothing as nice as watching a man enjoying himself by making his wife happy.

After that Elissa moved with easy charm through the lively crowd, one eye on the clock as it slowly crawled toward seven. Her sense of anticipation grew in vast leaps as the magic hour approached, and it lent an added fillip of excitement to the evening that was new to her. Soon, she told herself every two minutes or so, soon . . . "Elissa!"

She turned to smile at Martin approaching with a drink in his hand, his jacket unbuttoned over the slight paunch at his waistline. His dark looks were little marred by the signs of good living, however, and the thinning hair at the crown of his head was barely noticeable.

"I can't thank you enough for all this," he announced gratefully, waving a hand to encompass the successful party. "June was thrilled. She's never had a surprise party before. She's like a little girl with a new toy tonight," he went on delightedly.

"Don't thank me." Elissa grinned. "It was a brilliant idea on your part, and you know I love to entertain."

He nodded, not disputing the statement that the idea had been his. A lot of people came up with brilliant ideas around Elissa Sheldon. "Listen," he said, his features sobering as he talked. "I got the word about Evelyn late yesterday afternoon. I wanted you to know I'm sorry you didn't get the job. You deserved it and you would have been perfect for it." The brown eyes watched her glinting blue-green gaze for a moment. "Are you upset about it? I mean, Taggert hasn't been here very long and he likes to do things his own way. He probably made his choice without sufficient input . . ."

"I'm sure he had excellent reasons for his decision, and you're not to worry about me, Martin," Elissa admonished firmly. "No career ever advances straight up without one or two setbacks, and it's a good experience for me, I'm sure." She laughed with an ease she really didn't feel. Five more minutes, assuming Taggert would be on time. Somehow she was certain he would be. The wolf in him would be wanting to collect his prey.

"I'm glad you're taking it so well," Martin said, looking relieved. "I don't mind telling you Evelyn's going to need some help from you for the first couple of months. She's got ability, but she lacks your experience."

"Don't worry, she'll be welcome to all the assistance I can provide," Elissa promised, meaning it. Across the room, Dean looked up from his conversation with a woman who worked in Elissa's editing group and smiled. She returned the small intimacy and was about to excuse herself from the little conference with Martin when the doorbell rang.

For an instant Elissa froze. In spite of all the anticipation and the planning, she abruptly realized she wasn't totally prepared for the next few minutes. Quite belatedly she acknowledged to herself that Wade Taggert was a very unknown factor. Unlike the others in the room, who responded so readily to her charm, Taggert had already proved his resistance to it. He might want her, but he wasn't exactly *charmed* by her, she thought wryly, shaking off the momentary paralysis and going toward the door.

She hesitated once more before opening it, taking a deep breath and letting the anticipation flow through her. Few others in the crowd had paid any attention to the bell summons, and when Elissa mastered her suddenly trembling fingers sufficiently to unlock the door, most didn't even glance toward the newcomer. Whoever it was would be drawn into the cheerful group soon enough under Elissa's expert guidance.

Wade Taggert, as expected, dominated the hall outside the door. Dressed in a dark green pullover sweater and close-fitting slacks, he looked no less formidable than he did in the more formal suit and tie Elissa had always seen him in at the office. What

Elissa hadn't expected, for some strange reason, was the flash of hungry, glittering intent in the silvery gaze. She had known deep down that it would be there, just as she had known enough to expect the stern, harsh set of his mouth and the aura of unruffled power around him because she had seen them yesterday in his office. What she hadn't fully expected was to find them more intimidating than ever when the man stood at her threshold, waiting to step into her life.

To her own private disgust, Elissa felt her breath catch in her throat as his eyes clashed with hers. He didn't look beyond her into the room full of people. It was as if he had no curiosity whatsoever about the change in his plans for the evening. His whole attention was focused on Elissa's challenging, upturned face as she stood poised with one hand on the doorknob and one braced against the jamb.

"A party, Elissa?" he drawled with a deceptive mildness which didn't fool her at all. "You amaze me. I had assumed you'd want discretion to be the keyword for our little arrangement. I had no idea you intended to celebrate." The darkness of his hair gleamed in the hall light as he waited for her response with a taunting nonchalance which rasped along her nerve endings.

"Not a celebration, Wade," she murmured coolly, facing him with the sum total of her self-possession. "More of an object lesson for you on the perils of leaping to conclusions!"

"Are you sure it's a lesson you're trying to teach me, or did you organize all this with the idea of providing yourself with an illusion of safety while you negotiate? I thought I made it clear yesterday there's no point in bargaining with me. I hold the high cards in this little game." There was no threat in his words, only a calm statement of fact. Wade Taggert was very, very sure of himself.

"And in a few minutes when you realize you were completely wrong about me there will be no need to negotiate at all," she assured him, lifting her chin in a small, regal gesture. "Except, perhaps, when we discuss the nature of your apology. I'm assuming you will have enough integrity to want to do that, but I could be wrong. You may simply slink off into the night, unable to face me after you're forced to admit the truth."

"You're going to play this scene right out to the end, aren't you?" he noted with mocking admiration as he stepped forward, forcing her back into the room. For the first time he glanced around at the other guests, a few of whom were beginning to notice his presence.

Elissa was acutely aware of the astonished silence that descended briefly on the room as word went through the group that Wade Taggert had arrived. The others must be flabbergasted that she had invited the man who had denied her the well-earned promotion.

And for the first time in years there was an awkward stretch of silence at an Elissa Sheldon party. A silence she moved instinctively to deal with before it ruined June's celebration. Whatever her private battle with the tall, cold man at her side, her guests would not be involved.

"Look who managed to drop by, after all, everyone," she announced brightly, her fingers hovering lightly on the sleeve of Wade's sweater as she forced herself to lead him forward in a welcoming fashion. When his other hand came up to cover hers, clamping it to his forearm in a possession which to others might have appeared to be only a casually polite move, she realized she was trapped. The single option available to her now was to continue with her plan.

"Where's our guest of honor?" Elissa demanded cheerfully, searching the crowd for June's neat, dark head. "Ah, there you are.

Come and meet your husband's boss. Martin, I didn't want to tell you Mr. Taggert might drop by in case he couldn't make it . . ."

"Oh, there was never any doubt that I'd get here," Wade demurred, bending his head politely to a smiling June Randolph and releasing his grip on Elissa's hand to take the other woman's fingers in his. Elissa wisely used the momentary freedom to jerk her own hand off his sleeve and safely out of reach.

"I'm so happy to meet you," June chattered, unaware of the constraint in the room. "You're just in time to have a piece of birthday cake. I'm going to cut it in a moment."

"Thank you," Wade said softly, glancing at Martin Randolph, who stood behind his wife. "I believe this was to have been a surprise party for your wife?" he commented in an even tone which alerted Elissa at once.

"June's first one." Martin chuckled, putting an affectionate arm around her shoulders.

"And a complete success! I had no idea Elissa and Martin had been plotting," June grinned, slanting a happy look at her husband.

"I'm sure they worked very hard on it. It

appears to have gone off quite well," Wade said dryly, his gray eyes gliding over Elissa's carefully composed smile like a shark considering its next meal.

In spite of herself, she shivered, keeping the charming smile in place at a considerable cost. Bravely she challenged him with a mockingly raised eyebrow. Surely he must be getting the picture. June and Martin were clearly very much in love, and the excuse of planning a surprise party had been shown to be completely truthful. How long before he backed down? Elissa wondered, running an unconscious tongue tip over her lower lip in expectation. And how gracious would she allow herself to be when the time came to accept his apology? She was certain now she wouldn't allow him to escape without one.

"I was just going to bring out the cake," she declared, slipping lightly through the crowd toward the kitchen. The brief conversation with the Randolphs seemed to be breaking the brittle moment nicely. Others in the group who knew Wade and worked for him closed around him with polite, mildly curious greetings. He was still something of a stranger in the midst, she realized, stepping into the kitchen and picking up the beautifully constructed cake. Most of his employees had seen Wade only in brief, formal sessions at work. Finding him a part of their social world was bound to stimulate curiosity.

"Need any help, love?" Dean stuck his head around the corner and smiled.

"I think I can manage. Would you mind bringing that knife along, though?"

He picked it up obligingly. "So that's Taggert, hmm? The one who didn't give you the job?"

"That's the one, I'm afraid." She chuckled wryly.

"He's a little different from what I expected," Dean began slowly.

The voice which responded to the comment wasn't Elissa's. It was Wade's dark, heavy tones, and she whirled in surprise to see him lounging in the kitchen doorway, arms folded across his chest as he watched the other two.

"What, exactly, did you expect?" he asked the younger man a bit too gently.

"Never mind," Elissa commanded immediately, stepping between the two men, cake in hand. "We've got more important things to do right now. Bring that knife, Dean, and you, Wade, bring those extra napkins over there."

She moved forward with the attitude of a queen leading a procession and hoped she was leaving the men nothing else to do but follow obediently behind.

A chorus of oohs and aahs greeted the arrival of the cake, and June was pushed cheerfully forward to cut it. Dean graciously handed over the knife, and out of the corner of her eye Elissa could see Wade standing aloofly to one side, a handful of napkins clasped rather incongruously in his fingers.

"Now, this," Elissa began dramatically, "is a very special cake, June. Might I suggest you make the first cut about here?" She guided the woman's poised hand to a point over a pink rose. "Yes, I think that's about right. I would also suggest you cut very carefully."

There was a burst of laughter over the elaborate cake-cutting directions, and Martin shushed everyone with a wave of his hand. "This is very serious, folks," he joked and eyed his wife with mock warning. "Make that cut exactly as Elissa suggests, June!"

"You've both got me terrified of a simple cake," June complained laughingly, nevertheless sinking the knife into the icing with proper care. "I don't see what could be so difficult . . ." She paused a second later as the knife refused to continue its downward progress. "What in the world . . . ?" She bent over slightly to peer at whatever was impeding the knife's efforts. "Good heavens! There's something in here!"

Excited chattering and laughter urged her to finish the task, and poor June was nearly pushed into the icing as the other guests crowded in to see the grand surprise of the evening. A moment later June extracted a small plastic bag, the cake crumbs which clung to the outside failing to obliterate the glitter from within.

"Oh, my God!" June breathed as she held the plastic package in both hands and simply stared at it. Then her delighted, unbelieving eyes went to her proud husband. "Martin, you didn't! I can't believe it!"

Elissa stepped back out of the way as Martin moved close to his wife to accept her grateful kiss. The diamond necklace inside the plastic wrapper was released and passed around the room as tiny tears of pleasure trickled down the guest of honor's cheeks.

"A nice touch," Wade murmured, coming up behind Elissa's shoulder and keeping his voice so low that only she could hear it. "You were quite determined to prove me wrong tonight, weren't you, witch?"

She shrugged, not without a sense of satisfaction. "You wouldn't listen to me yesterday. But I figured even you couldn't ignore the evidence of your own eyes. And this sort of visual proof is the only thing you trust, isn't it?"

"You look extraordinarily pleased with yourself, Elissa Sheldon," he growled softly. She didn't turn around to look at him, keeping her attention on the furor the necklace was causing as it moved through various hands. But she could feel his massive presence behind her, and the image of a stalking wolf again came to mind. "I suppose," he went on coolly, "that you're expecting an apology? Or did you think I'd tell Evelyn she couldn't have the job, after all?"

Elissa did turn around at that, shocked. "Don't be ridiculous!" she charged, her eyes flashing at the suggestion. "You can't possibly take that job away from her. No, an apology is the only thing I expect to get out of this mess, Mr. Taggert. But by rights it ought to be a good one!"

"You expect me to get down on my knees?" he drawled interestedly, watching her with a deliberately provocative twist to his lips.

"That wouldn't be overdoing it one bit!" she vowed, aware of the excitement sparking through her as they neared the final confrontation.

"You'd be satisfied with that?" he mocked.

"Since I can hardly call you out for pistols at dawn, I shall have to be satisfied."

"In the old days defending a woman's honor was the responsibility of the man who protected her," Wade commented silkily, his eyes flicking briefly across the room to where Dean was busy admiring the necklace together with someone else. "I take it you're not going to sic your friend Dean on me?"

"I wouldn't think of involving him in this disgusting matter. Besides, I can take care of myself, Mr. Taggert," Elissa told him coldly.

"Tell me something," he invited almost casually, his eyes once again on her challenging gaze. "Have you been looking forward to the grand denouement all day long?"

"I've been looking forward to it since it first occurred to me to invite you over here so that you could see how wrong you'd been," she assured him tauntingly.

"In that case, I wouldn't want to spoil matters by acting precipitately," he retorted calmly. "I'll wait until after the party to let you know what I think of your efforts. In the meantime you can pour me a drink. I'm really not much of a birthday-cake eater." He pushed the napkins he'd been holding into one of her hands and then took her wrist firmly between steel fingers and forced her along to the bar she had arranged at the far end of the room.

There was nothing to do but allow herself to be dragged in his wake, Elissa realized with an inner sigh. She had no intention of creating a scene at her own party, and she would, after all, be getting her payment shortly.

That thought was enough to keep her going for the rest of the evening as the party sailed into high gear and eventually began to wind down. The leavetaking was reluctant on almost everyone's part, but eventually people did glance at their watches in resignation and began moving slowly out the door. Elissa saw each off on a rising tide of excitement, which dimmed only momentarily when she realized it was going to be awkward saying good-night to Dean Norwood, who was one of the last to leave.

"I'm not sure I like leaving you alone with that guy," Dean whispered at the door. He nodded his head surreptitiously toward a large chair where Wade sprawled, whiskey in hand, and appeared to study one of Elissa's strange paintings on the wall across from him.

"It'll be all right," she whispered back. "He just wants to discuss a business matter with me. He'll be leaving almost immediately."

"Are you sure?"

"Very," she breathed confidently.

"Do you think he's changed his mind about giving the job to that other woman?" Dean wondered vaguely, a small frown still drawing his brows together.

"I'm not certain, but it probably has something to do with my future at the company." She put a hand on his shoulder and lifted her lips for his kiss.

"Good night, love," Dean said, edging politely out the door. "It was a great party, as usual. I'll give you a call in a couple of days, okay?" He glanced uncertainly once more in Wade's direction. The other man ignored him completely. Rudeness came easily to Wade Taggert, Elissa decided.

"That will be fine, Dean."

With a last reassuring smile she closed the door on the remainder of her guests. Then, drawing a deep, anticipatory breath, Elissa turned and leaned back against the wood, her hands behind her on the knob, and waited for the satisfying conclusion to the evening.

Wade stirred in his chair, but he made no move to look at her. Instead he raised the glass of whiskey to his mouth, took a long swallow, and set it down on the table beside him.

"Well, Elissa," he said after a moment, and she straightened away from the door, prepared, she suddenly realized, to take an attitude of gracious hauteur.

"Yes, Wade?" she prompted coolly, coming forward slowly to receive the apology she had waited for so long. Her blue-green eyes gleamed with an unaccustomed brightness as she paused in front of him.

But his next words took her breath away with their sheer audacity, leaving her speechless as she met the dry ice of his eyes.

"You've put it off for an entire evening, but the time has come to give me my answer. I'm waiting, little witch. No more games."

"Your answer!" she finally managed, stunned. She stared at him, in bewilderment and rising anger. "What answer? I'm waiting for the apology you owe me, damn it! Why else would I have invited an overbearing, egotistical, rude male such as you to my party in the first place?"

"Because you thought you could fool me into thinking you'd been telling the truth about your relationship with Martin Randolph. Oh, it was all nicely staged, Elissa, but I'm not a complete idiot, you know. I realize the party has been a convenient cover for you and Martin, but don't expect me to buy the whole illusion!"

He moved, surging out of his chair and reaching out to snag her wrists in one hand. The cold flames of his eyes lashed her as he pulled her incredulous face close to his. "So let's have it, Elissa, my sweet witch. Have you made up your mind to accept a new lover in your life, or do you still need convincing?"

Chapter 3

"You," Elissa stated with great certainty, "must be out of your mind! Crazy! How did a crazy man ever get to be the manager of CompuDesign, for God's sake?"

"By a lot of hard work," Wade retorted, and for the first time since she'd met him, Elissa could have sworn an ingredient very close to humor stirred for an instant in the gray eyes. It was gone almost at once, but not before it had managed to catch her attention. She didn't tell herself she'd been mistaken. Elissa Sheldon knew people too well to think herself mistaken in a matter like that.

"You're hurting my wrists," she pointed out grittingly. "Would you mind letting me go? I'm not going to run anywhere. In case you weren't aware of the fact, this is my apartment!" She tossed her head in a small gesture of infuriated disdain. The dark red-highlighted hair moved gracefully, like the rippling coat of an animal.

"You're not accustomed to being hurt, are

you?" Wade observed laconically, glancing down at the slender wrists he was holding prisoner.

"I most certainly am not!" she agreed fervently, wriggling her fingers suggestively. But he didn't release them. Instead he seemed to lose interest in the cause of her protest, continuing to chain her in front of him with idle ease as his gleaming eyes moved back to her taut face.

"Think of it as a new and educational experience," he advised dryly. "Or perhaps as an object lesson, such as the one you tried to give me tonight!"

"You don't seem to have learned much from what I was trying to teach you!" she snapped, beginning to plot various ways of scratching out his eyes as soon as she had the use of her hands.

"I wouldn't say that," he disagreed mildly. "I learned, for example, just how incredibly charming you really can be. How many women, I wonder, go out of their way to give parties for their lover's wife?"

"Martin Randolph is not my lover! How many times do I have to tell you?"

"He won't be any longer, I'll grant you that." Wade smiled with dangerous promise. "As I told you yesterday, while I'm in your inner circle I won't tolerate any other man

65

sharing it with me. But even if I hadn't decided to find out for myself what's behind the bewitching facade you present to the world, I still think poor Randolph would have been shown the door. He had, after all, outlived his usefulness, hadn't he? He failed to get you that promotion."

"What a ghastly thing to say!" Elissa hissed. "Martin is a friend of mine, and he will continue to stay a friend!"

"That's the amazing thing, isn't it?" Wade nodded thoughtfully. "He probably will continue to be your friend. In fact, he'll probably come up with the notion that it was all his idea to break off the more intimate relationship and go back to being just friends. I could see from the way he acted with his wife tonight that already he's thinking about his marriage again. You're a very clever woman, my dear."

"He never stopped thinking about it!" Elissa shut her eyes in brief despair and disgust: "What's the point of arguing? You've made up your mind, and all the proof in the world won't change it, will it?"

"Who was going to be next on your list?" Wade persisted, and Elissa felt his fingers tighten further around her bruised wrists. "The stockbroker you had a little trouble getting rid of tonight? Norwood?"

And then a very strange thing happened in Elissa's mind. She allowed the raw frustration and rage seething inside to take control for a few short seconds, long enough to grate a scathing response to his demand.

"Yes," she heard herself say. "As a matter of fact, Dean is next on the list. Very good-looking, don't you think? Also quite successful. I might do more than charm him into bed — I might charm him into marriage!"

"I don't doubt for one minute that, left to your own devices, you could do exactly that," Wade growled. "But, as of tonight, you are no longer your own boss, free to glide through the world like some sort of sorceress, causing any man to whom you take a fancy to roll over and play dead or leap to do your bidding. You have power, Elissa Sheldon, but, unlike everyone else, I'm fully aware of it, and I'm going to see to it that you exercise some control in its use."

"You mean that I'm going to use it the way you want it used!" she said heatedly, wondering how she had ever gotten into such a devastating conversation.

"Now you're getting the idea," he approved, separating her wrists and enclosing one in each of his hands. Very deliberately, as if defying her to break free, he twisted her hands behind her back, arching her resisting softness against him. "Don't worry," he went on softly. "I wouldn't dream of trying to crush your enchantments. I only intend to see to it that you practice them on me for a while."

Elissa turned her head frantically to avoid the plundering of his mouth, but it was impossible. He held her too firmly, too closely, and there were no avenues of escape. His lips moved hungrily on hers, bruising her when she tried to fight him, softening seductively when she ceased struggling. The cycle of his attack was at once unswerving and inevitable. Elissa felt her senses begin to swim with the hopelessness of trying to break out of the circle. Each attempt at freeing herself brought only a punishing intensity in his kiss. Passiveness brought forth a gentler, intriguing exploration of her mouth.

"It's called conditioned response," Wade told her on a note of victorious masculine humor. "Soon you'll realize it's much more pleasant to stop fighting altogether."

"I want you to leave, Wade," Elissa tried ordering in desperation. She had to get rid of the man, and soon. There was a compelling danger in his embrace, and she was woman enough to recognize it. It weakened her with its sense of inevitability, but sought the embrace in the first place. And that was a very novel situation for Elissa Sheldon. Past romances had always been of a very *comfortable* nature, deftly managed by her with unerring instinct for what she liked to think was the benefit of both parties. She was not at all accustomed to being taken by storm, and she had no intention of growing used to the idea.

"But I'm not ready to leave," he whispered. "We have a great deal to discuss, you and I. Come over to the couch and I'll show you." With that he stepped back, retaining only a casual hold on her arm, and began to lead her toward the fat, pillowy sofa.

Elissa knew she wasn't going to get a better opportunity. She was dealing with a desperate situation, and it called for desperate remedies. Heart pounding, she allowed herself to be reluctantly dragged past the bar she had arranged earlier, now cluttered with used glasses and bottles. Appalled at her own daring, she reached out and snagged the nearest bottle.

You couldn't attempt this sort of thing with a faint heart, she challenged herself bracingly, and you had to do it quickly while there was still an element of surprise. Already Wade had turned to glance back in annoyance to see what was happening. She wouldn't aim for his head, she reassured her queasy stomach. Only his shoulder. The cloth of his sweater would protect him from being cut, but the impact should startle him enough to loosen his hold on her for a vital second or two. . . .

Her hand clutching the bottle was moving in an arc as the gray eyes collided with hers over his shoulder. In that instant she knew he realized what she was about to do and that she hadn't gotten enough of a head start. He would put out his free hand and catch her arm before the bottle found its target!

But he didn't. With sudden horror Elissa became aware that Wade was simply going to stand there and let her crack a half-full bottle of bourbon across his shoulder. The ice in his gaze dared her to go through with it, but she knew she couldn't. Not possibly!

It didn't take much to halt the blow before it landed. Elissa recognized that the effort had been rather half-hearted from the beginning, and the knowledge increased her fury severalfold. What was the matter with her? Had she no spirit whatsoever?

Still clutching the bottle by its neck, Elissa lowered her hand to her side and stood her ground grimly as Wade dropped her wrist and turned fully around to face her. There was a baiting attitude in him which was reflected in the wicked curve of his mouth and the narrowed gray eyes.

"Don't look so disgusted with yourself, little witch," he murmured, surveying her defiant glare and the unused weapon at her side. "I could have told you violence isn't your style. You're more at home with magic than you are with physical methods of attack."

"Unlike you!" she shot back daringly, regaining a measure of confidence as she realized he was no longer holding her.

The curve of his mouth widened, and he nodded agreeably. "Unlike me. If that bottle of bourbon had landed, there would have been hell to pay, Elissa Sheldon. You were very wise to think twice before you went through with the plan."

She eyed him scornfully. "Why? What would you have done? Beaten me?"

"With the greatest enthusiasm," he affirmed laconically. "You wouldn't have been able to sit down for a week."

Elissa eyed him with a new thoughtfulness as she hoisted the bourbon and set it on the bar. "Why didn't you try to stop me? So much simpler than messing about with a lot of broken glass!"

He shrugged. "A calculated risk. I didn't expect you to go through with it, and you didn't. The advantage of letting you find out for yourself that you couldn't do it was worth the risk."

"What an insufferable creature you are," Elissa breathed wonderingly. "I can't imagine how you've survived this long. You must have a great many enemies, Wade Taggert."

"Possibly, but I don't intend to count you among them," he informed her quite gently. "Besides, you never make enemies. You make it a point to charm everyone you meet, don't you? Has it always been easy for you? I'll bet you were born with the ability."

"Too bad the same can't be said of you! I've never met a less charming man in my life!" she glazed, flushing under his accusation that she somehow used her many friends.

"No, I haven't gotten where I am by enchanting everyone around me," he allowed easily. "I've fought for everything I've ever wanted. It's a different way of getting what one wants out of life than the method you've employed, but effective, nevertheless."

Elissa saw the mockery in him as he watched her, and she found herself wanting to flatten him. "It might be effective but I'd rather have people like me than think of me as a wolf!"

"Is that how you see me?" he demanded with great interest.

"Yes," she confirmed with relish. "A lone wolf, taking what you want out of life with no regard for anyone else. A predator! That's what you reminded me of tonight, trying to socialize a little, put people at ease as if they were sheep you wanted to calm. But it never quite works, does it? People may relax a bit, even try some casual conversation with you, but a part of them is always slightly wary. Their instincts tell them the wolf is still there under the surface."

"But even big bad wolves want some kindness in their lives, Elissa," he muttered in a new, lower, almost purring tone as he lifted a hand to touch a finger to the line of her jaw. "Just because I see your sorcery for what it is doesn't mean I'm immune to it, you know. For over a month, since the first day I saw you, in fact, I've been giving you opportunities to draw me into your web and try your charms on me, but you've always ignored me. Is it any wonder I finally decided to take matters into my own hands?"

"What in the world are you talking about?" she yelped, astounded. "You and I have rarely crossed paths since the day you arrived!"

"Only because you kept avoiding me. Every time I tried to create an opportunity for you to get to know me, you acted oblivious to my bait."

"If you're talking about the afternoon you called me into your office to discuss the career paths for the various members of my writing group . . ." she began heatedly, thinking of that short, businesslike meeting.

"I am." He smiled quirkingly. "You came totally prepared with case histories on everyone who reports to you, spent half an hour extolling their virtues, and left without even giving me a chance to get a word in edgewise."

"You'd made it clear you wanted a concise report, and that's what I gave you!" she snapped, incensed.

"I had intended," he informed her dryly, "to extend the discussion through cocktails at my place, but you raced in and out of my office like a whirlwind. Then there was the morning I stopped you in the hall and suggested I get to know more about the writing group over lunch. I thought I was making progress until you showed up at the appointed time and place with the five writers you supervise."

Elissa reddened, remembering the occasion. "They were all thrilled by your interest," she mumbled, her eyes lowering self-consciously to the knot of his tie.

"Tell me something," he urged, lifting her chin between thumb and forefinger. "You didn't really misunderstand my invitation that morning, did you? You deliberately chose to interpret it as meaning I wanted to take the whole group out to lunch. Why, Elissa? I've seen you turn a corner at the end of a hall just to avoid having to walk past me!"

"That's not true," she defended, thoroughly irritated at his perception and at herself for having allowed her instinctive avoidance response to show. She had found herself going out of her way to forestall small encounters, and she had purposely misinterpreted his invitation to lunch. Exactly why she had done so wasn't entirely clear to her on the various occasions involved, but now she knew. Her feminine instincts had been working overtime, warning her of a new kind of danger in her life — warning her of a man who couldn't be handled the way she automatically handled other men.

"It is true!" he countered. "But why me, Elissa? Why haven't I qualified for your magic circle? You didn't even invite me to your last party even though most of the rest of the staff went, and I understand my predecessor always had a standing invitation to your parties."

"Don't act as if you're some poor waif from the storm to whom I've refused shelter and comfort," she snarled, jerking herself away from his touch on her face and stepping a pace out of reach.

"You've known from the beginning that even if you could succeed in charming me, you'd never be able to make the thorough job of it that you do on others, isn't that right?" he pressed, closing the space between them but not touching her again. The gray flames of his eyes swept her outraged face. "You'd never be able to dazzle me to such an extent that I wouldn't be aware of how little of you I was really getting. I'll always know if I'm being short-changed, witch, and I won't tolerate it. Wolves aren't noted for taking less than their full share. And I do want my share, honey," he added in suddenly cajoling tones. "I want to have your softness and your wide-eyed, fascinated interest and have you remember the way I like my drinks and all the rest. Surely you can understand that? I'm only a man, Elissa, and I want to be charmed like the others. . . ."

"Don't give me that line," Elissa grated furiously. "I've read Little Red Riding Hood!"

"Then you know the wolf got everything he wanted in the end."

"This time the story is going to have a different conclusion, Wade Taggert!" she vowed, trying to stifle the leap of her pulses as she confronted this new and dangerous element in her life. It would be the height of folly to allow the intrigue of the situation to pull her under. She knew, deep inside, she might never resurface.

"No," he denied in deep, blighting tones. "It's not. I'm going to get what I want, too. Even though I'm going to have to reach out and take it for myself instead of having you give it to me. But that's all right. I'm used to doing things that way. And before you and I are through, Elissa Sheldon, I'm going to have everything. Not just the bits and pieces you bestow so sweetly on others, but the part that no one ever even gets close to. . . ."

"What are you talking about?" she blazed, a strange and curious fear licking down her spine.

"I'm talking about the part of you that goes into your paintings," he tossed back with casual ruthlessness.

Elissa swallowed tightly. "My paintings?"

she repeated distantly. No one had ever guessed she was the creator of the unearthly landscapes. No one had even asked if she had painted them. Everyone just assumed she had the idiosyncrasy she claimed to have where art was concerned, and people promptly forgot about the subject as soon as Elissa had gently turned them aside from it. Yet this man who hardly knew her and who had never been in her apartment before tonight had instantly recognized them as her work.

"Did you think I didn't know you'd done them?" he asked in some surprise, seeing the bafflement and wariness in her face. "But of course I knew." He frowned, shaking his head at her obtuseness. A flicker of understanding flashed across the hard planes of his face, and then he smiled very slightly. "But others don't know, do they? And if they did, they wouldn't understand. Just as they don't understand why you have such things hanging in your apartment in the first place. Most people would be floored to know you'd painted them yourself. After all, they're so *unlike* you, honey," he drawled mockingly.

"What's that supposed to mean? There's nothing wrong with those paintings!"

"Except that they reveal a side of you no

one has ever had the sense to see was there," he whispered huskily. "The side of you I'm going to take, along with all the rest of you!"

Once more Elissa stepped back, but this time she was too slow and he caught her before she could get out of reach.

"No!" she snapped, slapping at his hand as he used it to pull her close. His arm moved, but only to form a cradle with his other one as he swooped and lifted her off her feet with soft violence. "Wade!" she protested, genuinely alarmed now. "Put me down this instant! I won't have you treating me as if . . . as if . . ."

"As if I own you?" He grinned daringly, stalking across to the overstuffed sofa and tossing her lightly down into it. Before she could scramble aside, he was sprawling on top of her, anchoring her beneath him. "But that's the way it's going to be, little witch," he went on beguilingly, his rough palms framing her infuriated features. "You wouldn't take me into your world willingly, so I'm going to make a place for myself there."

"Not a chance!" she got out between gritted teeth. "I've got news for you: my job doesn't mean that much to me! Certainly not enough to convince me to be your mistress!" She could feel the weight of him along the length of her and was vaguely amazed at the latent demand she sensed in that heaviness.

"You're not such a coward as to quit merely because you've learned the price you'll pay for holding on to your position," he taunted, the thumbs of his hands probing the corners of her mouth intimately.

"It's not a question of cowardice, damn you!"

"Are you admitting you don't have sufficient power to charm me into giving you what you want?" he retorted gently, challengingly. "Come, no, Elissa, just because everything's been so easy for you up until I appeared on the scene, that's no reason to quit at the fist sign of trouble."

"Don't you dare make fun of me," she breathed tightly, aware of her helplessness and painfully aware of the sensual tension enveloping them both. "Your behavior is utterly despicable! Any man who would use his position to try and force one of his female employees to sleep with him is beneath contempt!"

"No more so than a woman who uses her body to get what she wants!"

"Wade, I swear I never did such a thing!" she tried frantically. "I invited you here tonight to try and prove it to you. Since you refuse to believe the only evidence I have, you leave me no choice but to quit my job!"

"Suit yourself," he rasped. "There are some pretty obvious benefits in the deal for you if you stay on at CompuDesign, but leaving the company's not going to get rid of me. I know what I want, and every day that passes makes me more certain." He relaxed slightly. "But you want your job. Admit it."

She heard the absolute promise in his voice and sucked in her breath. "You can't *hound* me, Wade! I won't have it!" she wailed.

"I'm not going to hound you, sweet witch," he vowed, bending his head to find the hollow of her throat under the lacy collar of her blouse. "I'm going to make love to you. Every chance I get!"

Once more Elissa drew in her breath sharply, but this time for a different reason. Try as she would, and as dangerous as she knew it to be, she could not build up sufficient resistance to the overwhelming demand emanating from him. There was a fire on her skin everywhere his mouth descended, and he used his weight to force an intimate, electric contact against her hips.

Elissa had one brief moment of hope when he abruptly elevated himself for a few seconds, but the respite lasted only long enough for him to angle her more directly beneath him, and then she found herself crushed again into the cushions of the sofa.

"Wade! Please!" she begged as one of his hands began to explore her body with arousing hunger.

He silenced her protest with his mouth, fastening it on hers in carefully controlled ferocity that demanded entrance for the invasion of his tongue. She lost the battle to keep him out when he used his teeth with delicate savagery on her vulnerable lip. She gasped at the implied pain which was not yet pain, and he used the short weakness in her defenses to taste the warm honey behind her lips.

Simultaneously with the unlocking of her mouth Wade's hand closed possessively over her small breast, and she felt the tremor that went through both of them at the contact. Elissa sensed the rising tide of the assault and began to panic at her own inability to stem it.

There was need and demand and desire and promise in the way Wade's fingers left her breast momentarily to seek the buttons of her blouse. His mouth slid moistly across hers, withdrawing from one conquered territory to search out another. He found it in the sensitive tip of her earlobe just as his probing fingers found the entrance to her blouse.

"Sweet witch," he husked as he toyed luxuriously with the earlobe he had captured. "You're so good at knowing what others need. You wouldn't turn me away at the gate, would you? Not when I need you more than the others do."

"You want too much," she cried softly, despairingly as her buttons gave beneath his efforts. The front clasp of her bra was soon dealt with, and then her flesh tingled unmercifully as he palmed the nipple he had been stalking.

"How could I want any less than all of you?" he demanded hoarsely. She shivered involuntarily and knew at once that he sensed it. Instantly, his fingertips tightened tantalizingly around the tip of her breast, coaxing forth the nipple as if luring a small creature from its burrow.

Elissa shut her eyes against the force of her own response, dazed at the impact he was having on her senses. Against her volition her hands freed themselves from where they had been wedged against his shoulders and went to the thick darkness of his hair. Cautiously at first and then with increasing urgency she slid her fingertips through the gray at his temples and on into the blackness beyond. She heard him groan in unrestrained hunger as her fists eventually settled at the nape of his neck, clenching and unclenching the muscles there.

He *did* want her, she thought in wonder. With a power she'd never sensed in other men. It was nearly impossible to imagine Dean Norwood, for example, demanding and forcing this level of response. But Dean Norwood was a civilized, polite human being who would be a gentleman even when he made love. Wade Taggert's needs and masculine desire went beyond the level of a gentleman's. And he had no inhibitions about letting her know the intensity of his demands, Elissa thought dimly, her mind whirling.

"Randolph and that damn stockbroker might be satisfied with what you choose to give them, and in the end, when you tire of them, they'll leave still thinking of themselves as your friends," Wade muttered fiercely as his lips began tracking down her throat to the curve of her breast. "But if and when our affair comes to an end, there will be no friendship between us, my witch! I can't look at you without wanting to posses you — and whatever happens, that element will never change!"

"Wade! You don't know what you're

saying!" And then Elissa's words were broken off in a gasp as his tongue found the tip of her gentle curve to replace the hand which had been at work there and had now moved on.

"Yes, I do." He grated against her breast as he traced a feathery pattern on the warm skin of her stomach. "I want to know the part of you living in that crumbling castle in your painting. The part that's protected by the dragons you've got hanging all around this apartment. You look out at the world from some inner sanctum and find the rest of us amusing little pets, don't you? But not me, Elissa," he vowed, lifting his head for a moment to rake her startled, tense face.

"I'm not a pet for you to gently, kindly, control and manipulate or please because it amuses you or because it keeps everything in your world flowing comfortably along. I'm the wolf you called me a few minutes ago, and I'm going to sit beside you in your castle, not beg outside the door! You'll pet me, Elissa, but no more often than I'll pet you. And in the end you'll be as chained in my power as I will be in yours."

"That's utterly absurd!" she managed, knowing the feel of hot honey flowing through her veins and appalled at it. "We're two very ordinary human beings, Wade! Not enchanters from another world who can cast spells over each other and see which of us is the stronger!" Her blue-green eyes had deepened in shading until they reflected the depths of a remote sea as she looked up into his uncompromising features.

"Shall I tell you your own great secret?" he asked musingly. "Will that prove my power is at least a match for your own?"

"What nonsense is this?" she hissed uncertainly, searching the gray gaze for some hint of his meaning.

"Your best-kept secret, little witch, and the source of your magic is that, in spite of all the friends and admirers you so easily cultivate, you could close the door on all of them tomorrow, retreat into your painting or read books of fantasy, and not miss any of them. You're completely self-contained inside the walls of your castle, aren't you? And no one even has a clue. Except for me, naturally," he added calmly, matter-of-factly.

Elissa was dumbfounded. The one remark which finally penetrated her reeling brain was the comment he'd made on the science fiction. "What do you know of my fantasy collection?" she charged, a new wave of fury roaring through her senses. She thought of the books on her shelf and winced.

He moved his hands back up to cup her face and smiled with patent triumph. "I wandered into your bedroom during the party. I wanted to see more after I saw the paintings."

"My bedroom!" For some unknown reason Elissa felt as if some part of her had been violated, invaded. "You took it upon yourself to do a thing like that? Haven't you ever heard of private property? What kind of person are you?"

"You've already decided I'm a predator. We wolves set out own boundaries." He grinned, clearly enjoying her shock and anger.

"I'm glad you're so damned pleased with yourself," she ripped at him violently.

"Calm down, Elissa," he ordered, the grin fading as he felt her tremble with the force of her anger. "I already knew there were mysteries about you. It was natural for me to go looking for them."

"And what are your secrets, Wade Taggert?" she asked fiercely, sea eyes narrowing with menace even though it would have been clear to any observer that she was in no position to threaten Wade. All the menace was plainly on his side.

"Secrets?" he repeated softly. "I don't have any secrets. Not from you. Only a need to be charmed. A need for you to want me, really want me, not just find me comfortable for a while. Is that so much to ask?"

Elissa couldn't believe the near wistfulness of his tone. His most dangerous tactic yet, she told herself grimly. She must not allow herself to be seduced by the depth of his desire and need. Who would have realized that she, of all people, would be in such danger from this aspect of the man? It didn't bear contemplation! Her head moved restlessly, negatingly, on the cushion as she continued to focus on the soundless gray pools of his eyes. He must have known of her chaotic thoughts, because his smile suddenly gentled in a way which was altogether new. And every bit as dangerous as his strength.

"Elissa, Elissa," he whispered, "I tried to work my way into your spells through normal routes; I tried to bribe my way in with promises of advancing your career, the one thing I thought might be important to you; I've demanded admission on my own terms. And now I'm asking very politely. I want to know your magic, little witch. Come be my woman and find out what it's like to put yourself in someone else's power for once. I promise you won't regret it, my sweet. I'll take good care of you . . ."

"The way you already took good care of

my promotion?" she snapped, trying to fight the weakness in herself and fearing failure.

"I had to do something to show you that you couldn't use Randolph to get what you want," he explained, as if to a small child to whom he had denied candy. "I'm the one who can make life difficult or pleasant for you, Elissa. And I might prove more complicated to manage than men like Randolph or Norwood. But think of the challenge!" he urged goadingly.

"You still think I tried to sleep my way into that position, don't you?" she muttered forlornly, not understanding how anyone could think that of her. No one ever thought the worst of Elissa Sheldon. Everyone who knew her would realize she wouldn't have dreamed of using sex to get that job.

"It doesn't matter now," he soothed, stroking her cheekbones with his fingers. "That lesson is over, and I won't allow you to stray again . . ." The cold rain in his eyes turned a deeper shade for an instant. "Except with me!"

"You want me in spite of what you think is my history of sneaky, underhanded, conniving behaviour, is that it?" she murmured disbelievingly. No one had ever thought the worst of her, but if someone had she certainly wouldn't expect him to pursue her so intently after learning the awful truth. What manner of man was Wade Taggert?

"I think you're salvageable," he informed her bluntly. "You've always worked your charms so easily that you've grown accustomed to using them to smooth your path through life. But I don't believe you're really bad. You require a firm hand and some guidance from a man who sees through your magic even while he's availing himself of it. And you need to find out what it's like to want a man so much that you couldn't just walk away and close the door on him!"

Chapter 4

Elissa closed her eyes against the astounding presumption of the man who still held her pinned against the couch and then she let her lashes flutter open very wide. "You think you're the man to keep me under control?" she drawled very coolly.

"I want you, Elissa," he stated categorically. "And that means I've got to control you, make you want me, or I'll find my fingers very badly burned, won't I?"

"The experience of getting yourself singed might be quite salutary," she offered bitterly.

She saw the reluctant smile touch his eyes and the edges of his mouth.

"I think I can take care of myself," he promised meaningfully. She could feel the certainty in him. It had a palpable presence. He was so sure he'd win. . . .

"And what's in all this for me?" she demanded a little too gently, feeling the rage mingle with the other new emotion she was experiencing tonight. Together they made a potent combination in her bloodstream.

"Your career back on track," he said immediately, not appearing the least reluctant to enumerate the material advantages of an association with him. "The challenge of finding out if you've met a man you can't ultimately control. I'm counting on that as a lure as great as advancing in your job, by the way." He smiled bleakly. "The temptation of discovering what passion can be with a man who doesn't think of himself as merely a good friend, and . . ." He hesitated and then said with shattering callousness, "Perhaps a necklace or two thrown in on the side. Something to make up for the one you had to give up to June tonight."

It was too much. Elissa knew she could no longer resist the risk of trying to bring the pompous, overbearing Wade Taggert down into the dust at her feet. Never had she experienced such violent feelings toward another human being, but, then, never had she been treated like this, either! If there was any justice in the universe she was going to bring it crashing around his ears!

But such a goal meant playing his repellent game very, very carefully, Elissa realized with surprisingly cold logic. She must lead him delicately, cleverly, to the point of final victory. And then hurl everything back in his face!

The punishment of Wade Taggert would be a new adventure for her, Elissa thought as her pulses pounded in anger and excitement. It would take her far out of the normal, comfortable routine of her life. The man would be as dangerous as any of the strange beasts in her paintings, and she would have only herself to blame if she got in over her head.

But the apology she had been seeking from him earlier in the evening had become a goal she couldn't ignore. In fact, she decided boldly, an apology alone would not be enough to satisfy her newly awakened craving for revenge. Not nearly enough!

"My career back on track . . ." she repeated thoughtfully, as if turning the idea over in her mind. "You give me your word to restore my promotion — or one equivalent to it, since you can't very well take the job away from Evelyn at this point?" She moistened her slightly parted lips in a faintly provocative gesture, her eyes wide and interested. Elissa had never set out to play a *femme fatale,* but every woman had a few instincts to fall back on in a crisis.

"Behave yourself and give me what I want, and I'll take care of everything," Wade promised with a pouncing effect in his voice. She could almost see his thoughts spinning out plans. He was so sure he had her, so sure that he'd found the key to her when he'd taken control of her future at CompuDesign.

"I'm . . . I'm not quite certain if I can trust you," Elissa hedged, allowing feminine caution to flicker in her searching gaze.

"You have my word," he told her arrogantly, as if that should be sufficient.

"But I hardly know you," she pointed out gently. "Perhaps your word is worthless . . ."

"You can trust me, Elissa," he told her with a sudden frown. She realized he wasn't used to having his word of honor questioned, and that gave her a great deal of encouragement.

"Perhaps," she mused baitingly. "Perhaps not. You're asking me to risk a lot, aren't you? A woman wants to have some faith in a man's intentions before she agrees to a situation like this. You've already told me I won't be able to count on charming you into completing your end of the bargain . . ." She let the words trail off suggestively, and his frown intensified. He hadn't expected this particular hitch, she thought gleefully.

"What are you recommending?" he demanded forcefully. "That I give you a promotion first? Before I collect what's owed me? I'm not that foolish, little witch!"

"I didn't expect you would be." She smiled placatingly. "I'm only going to suggest that we give ourselves some time to get to know each other before embarking on a full-scale affair. In spite of what you may think of me, I don't wander through life hopping from one bed to another!"

"Yesterday I gave you a day's grace to think the matter over, and I arrived for my answer tonight only to find you'd spent the time planning to prove me wrong. You didn't have any doubt you'd be successful, did you? Now you're asking for more time. Will I come back in a few days only to find you've erected other fortifications and defenses? I don't feel like wasting any more nights, Elissa," he concluded warningly. His hand moved to settle once more over her breast in flagrant possession.

She shivered involuntarily at the touch and took a firm grip on her nerves. "I'm not suggesting I spend the time in solitary thought about the matter, Wade. I'm offering to spend the time getting to know you. Is that so much to ask?" She knew she'd hit a vulnerable point when she'd expressed doubt in his word, and she homed in on it with intuitive accuracy. Elissa was good at diagnosing the weak points in others, but her automatic reaction when she located one was to treat it gently, kindly. To build and strengthen, not use the advantage. Tonight constituted one of the rare moments in her life when she deliberately hammered at a sensitive area in a man's ego. The last time she could clearly recall doing so was the time she had found a young boy mistreating a small dog. Her anger had caused her to rip the boy to shreds, reducing him to tears in a matter of minutes. Later she had been sorry, wishing she'd used positive instead of negative tactics to show him the error of his ways, and she'd made an effort to do so in other encounters.

But tonight she would think only of herself, she vowed silently, and that meant using every advantage she could garner.

"You'll spend the time only with me? No one else?" he verified as if going over the terms of a bargain. His palm scraped a little roughly on her delicate nipple, and Elissa realized he wasn't even aware of the tiny roughness.

"Yes, Wade." She nodded quickly, appealingly. "We'll . . . we'll treat it like the start of any normal romance, discovering each other, getting to know one another. A dating relationship."

"I hope you don't expect me to keep my hands completely off you during the course of this game," he mocked. But she could see the triumph still swirling in his eyes. He was sure he could handle everything.

"I expect you'll try to seduce me, but don't expect me to be easily persuaded into your bed." She couldn't keep the tartness out of her voice, but he didn't seem to mind.

"You won't allow that to happen until you're sure I can be relied upon to complete my end of the bargain, is that it?" he bit out. "In the end you'll come to me on faith alone, witch, because I'm not going to let you talk me into giving you the things you want until I've got what I want!"

"We shall see, won't we?" she murmured provokingly, lowering her dark auburn lashes so that he wouldn't see the look in her eyes.

"So it's a game you're playing!" Wade eyed her consideringly for an instant and then slowly, resolutely, lowered his head and kissed the small bones of her exposed shoulder with cool aggression. "Very well, witch," he grated against her skin, letting his mouth taste her. She could feel his tongue curl raspingly on her and had all she could do not to flinch from the barbaric caress. "I'll play your games with you," he told her challengingly, confidently. "You'll find I'm an opponent worthy of your best magic!"

97

"Then," she essayed boldly, "if we're agreed on the terms and conditions, it's time you left."

"Kicking me out already?" he mocked, making no effort to move his weight off her. The black brows climbed upward with quelling intimidation. "I've hardly begun to explore some of your most interesting secrets." His eyes holding hers, Wade slid his hand down the length of her rib cage to the waistband of her skirt.

"I want you to leave," Elissa demanded as her breath seemed to catch at the back of her throat. "You've got what you came for tonight . . ."

"Not quite," he contradicted, letting his fingers stray inside the waistband.

"Let me phrase that a little differently," she snapped. "You've got all you're going to get tonight!"

"I can see that even though you've lost this evening, your spirit isn't anywhere near crushed." He suddenly chuckled, a rich sound from deep in his chest. The gray eyes glinted with the awakened humor in him.

"Is that what you want? My spirit in tatters?"

"Oh, no," he denied at once. "Never that. I only want it controlled. Properly chained and controlled by me!"

"I learned a lesson about not counting chickens before they're hatched yesterday," Elissa said sweetly. "Perhaps you're due to learn the same thing."

He grinned savagely. "I knew you wouldn't be able to resist a challenge of suitable proportions."

"Your proportions are large, all right," she retorted. "You're crushing me!"

"Too bad." He sighed humorously, moving at last to sit up beside her on the couch. "I find you extremely comfortable." he watched as she hastily struggled to a sitting position and tried buttoning her blouse with shaking fingers. She wasn't certain if it was rage or sheer reaction which caused her to tremble, but it made the small task difficult.

"Here," he told her quite gently, "I'll do that."

"No!" she said waspishly, pushing his hands aside. "I want you to go, Wade. I've had enough of our little 'game' this evening!" She stopped trying to fasten the blouse and held the edges clutched tightly in her fingers, lifting resentful, defiant eyes to meet his.

"Yes," he agreed surprisingly, the hand he had been intending to use to help her with the blouse going to her hair and ruffling the now-tousled stuff with a tenderness which astonished Elissa. "I think you have had enough for tonight. It can't be a familiar experience for you to find yourself facing such complications in life. I suppose I should show some understanding, especially since I've won so heavily this evening. I'll go, Elissa, and leave you to retreat temporarily to your tower and consider the situation. But only for a short while. I shall be back tomorrow to shake the bars on your door again."

"What are you talking about?" she grumbled, pleased that he was going to leave without much more fuss but wary of his willingness to do so.

"Tomorrow is Sunday, and I'm going to spend it with you. Just as you suggested when you bargained for time a few minutes ago," he said, acting surprised that she hadn't expected him to be back in the morning.

Elissa's eyes slitted ever so slightly. Well, the game had to commence sometime. It might as well be tomorrow. How long, she wondered, would it take to bring this man to his knees? And what would constitute a proper penance? Not just an apology, not anymore. He'd had his chance to get away with that alone!

"What did you want to do tomorrow?" she asked loftily, trying to appear unconcerned.

He smiled. "I think I'll take you on a picnic."

"A picnic! That's impossible! You can't have a picnic in Seattle in the winter. It will be raining!"

"It won't be raining in my apartment," he tossed back, getting easily, lithely, to his feet.

She frowned, ignoring the hand he had stretched down to help her up beside him. "I'm not going to your apartment."

"Yes, you are," he told her significantly. "You're committed to the game, witch. There's no way out. If you want me to play within your rules for a while, you'll have to obey them yourself. And that means spending time with me. A great deal of time! We're supposed to be getting to know each other, remember?" he finished mockingly.

"I remember!" she flashed, incensed that he would imply she wasn't going to play fair. "What time will you pick me up?" she demanded rashly.

"A little before noon. Good night, Elissa, my sweet witch," he added, his voice darkening several shades as he tipped up her chin and feathered her lips with a kiss of off-

101

hand power. "Go off to your solitary bed and dream about the night when you'll have a wolf in your bedroom!"

Before Elissa could come up with a properly crushing retort, Wade was gone, smiling boldly as he strode toward the door and let himself out into the hall.

For a long moment she stood very still amid the aftermath of the party and stared at the door which had been closed so quietly behind her last, marauding guest. What had she let herself in for in her determination to punish Wade?

It was only as she was dumping soiled napkins into the garbage and thinking about the picnic to which she had been forcibly invited that a tiny, worrisome thought made its way to the forefront of Elissa's mind.

When all was said and done, Wade had left with rather more willingness than she would have expected in the situation. He had, after all, not believed her innocent of his accusations. In a sense, for him nothing had changed. Yet he had agreed quickly to her demand for time to get to know each other. Elissa paused in her work, frowning with an unpleasant suspicion.

What if, she asked herself grimly, Wade hadn't really expected her to leap straight into an affair even with the lures he thought he held, such as helping her career? What if his goal tonight had been only to assure a place in her life and make it impossible for her to ignore him as she had been doing for the past month? Had he demanded much, hoping for the compromise she had come up with herself?

Elissa slammed a stack of plates heavily on the counter, wincing as she thought she heard a crack from the one on the bottom. Surely she hadn't been so stupid as to allow herself to be manipulated!

No, she assured herself an instant later. Her own motives were clear. She was going into this strange and reckless game for one reason only: to make Wade eat his words. He would grovel at her feet before she was through with him! He wanted an affair with her, did he? One he controlled? Well, by the time she'd finished with him he would be humbling himself and begging for marriage!

That, she knew with a flash of sheer inspiration, was the proper punishment for Wade Taggert's crime. He would find himself begging to marry the woman he was convinced he could manipulate into an affair. Begging to marry the woman he thought was so unscrupulous she would sleep with a man in order to advance herself. How much pride would he have to swallow before he reached such a stage? Elissa wondered with mounting excitement. A great deal, no doubt!

And when that lovely moment arrived when Wade Taggert was pleading for her hand in marriage, she would coolly, mockingly, hurl his offer back in his teeth, together with the damn job he thought meant so much to her. She would crush that rampaging ego of his if it was the last thing she did!

A little shaken at the unfamiliar intensity of her emotions, Elissa went to bed.

Sunday dawned, as Elissa had predicted, cold and wet. But that was only to be expected of Seattle in the winter, and she went about her normal weekend routine without giving the matter much thought. It was difficult, she acknowledged honestly, to think of anything else except Wade Taggert, anyway.

What would have happened, she asked herself more than once as she sprawled on the couch with the Sunday paper and a cup of coffee, if she had invited Wade into her life in the beginning? If she had picked up one of the more conventional lures he had claimed he'd tried? Would they still have arrived at this juncture? The question was fairly academic, she decided wryly, turning to the comics first. Try as she would, she simply couldn't see herself as ever willingly inviting the man into her circle of friends. He just didn't fit the way others did. How could a wolf fit comfortably into her life?

Besides, she declared with silent conviction, there was something distinctly uncomfortable about being wanted as intently as Wade Taggert seemed to want her. She had never encountered anyone like him, and she was glad of that. But she couldn't keep her pulse running at a normal speed as noon approached.

Once again she was watching a clock and waiting for Wade, Elissa realized with dark humor as she checked her casually elegant designer jeans and silky sapphire-blue shirt in the hall mirror. The jeans fit like a glove, emphasizing the feminine curve of her hip and the sweep of her leg. The shirt had a dashing air in its style which left her throat bare to reveal the tiny gold chain she wore. The outfit suited her mood, she decided, a little bold and reckless. For a moment she envisioned herself on a pirate ship, cutlass in hand, a scarf rakishly tied around the flame of her hair. Yes, the clothes suited her mood.

The nervous tension raced into high throttle as the doorbell sounded a moment later, and Elissa braced herself mentally and physically as she opened the door.

Wade stood in the hall as he had done last night with the same hungry wolf gleam in his eyes. He was dressed as she was in jeans, but not the designer variety. His were the rugged, faded, lean sort which would have looked at home on the range and had plainly seen some action outside the city. There was a plaid flannel shirt to go with the jeans, and Wade had a weathered-looking suede jacket with fleece lining slung over his shoulder. He smiled broadly as he eyed the length of her.

"Is this the latest thing in Red Riding Hood outfits?" he drawled, the gleam in his gaze approving. Elissa could have sworn there was a lightness about his mood which she hadn't seen before, and she wondered if it was because he thought he held the winning hand.

"I would have thought a professional wolf would keep in touch with the latest fashions for visiting grandmother's house."

"In touch is exactly what I want to be when you're looking that tasty," he drawled outrageously, stepping forward and catching her close with a firm hand planted on the neatly outlined curve of her rear.

"Wade!" she gasped, a bit shocked by his audacity. "Behave yourself!" She frowned at him in ferocious warning which he appeared not to notice. Gingerly she stepped back out of reach.

"We wolves have our own code of behavior," he murmured, watching as she collected a leather jacket from the hall closet.

"A fascinating sociological study, no doubt," she gibed, telling herself there was nothing wrong in going along with his mood. She wanted him off guard, didn't she?

"I'll tell you all about it over lunch," he promised, stepping aside so that she could precede him through the door.

"Shall I take notes on the tablecloth in case there's a quiz later?" she inquired dryly as they waited for the elevator.

"That won't be necessary. I'll be happy to keep going over the fine points with you until you've learned the subject thoroughly."

In the lobby of the apartment building Elissa allowed him to help her on with her jacket, shrugging lightly into it and tying the belt. "Where's your car?" she asked, glancing out into the wet street.

"Over there. Only a short dash!" He chuckled.

"You're illegally parked!" she scolded as he pushed her out the door with an encouraging hand.

"I was counting on your being ready on time," he admitted, turning up the collar of his own jacket as they hurried through the mist. "And the fact that it's Sunday."

"Living dangerously, I see," she remarked, slipping into the passenger side of a sleek silver Jaguar which undoubtedly raised appreciative eyebrows on all those like herself fortunate enough to ride in it.

He slid into the seat beside her, filling the cockpit area with his massive presence, and turned to smile at her before starting the engine.

"You're the dangerous element in my life at the moment, witch. All other risks pale in comparison."

Suspense flashed along her nerves at the intimate, warning timbre of his voice, and it was all Elissa could do to keep her response pert.

"You're not trying to tell me you've reconsidered during the night and decided the whole game is too much for you! If you're so afraid of me we can call a halt right now."

"I'm not about to lose by default," he growled, putting the car in gear. "In fact, I'm not about to lose at all. I merely remarked that there is an element of risk involved."

"But you're convinced you'll get what you

want in the end?" she murmured with mocking curiosity, slanting a sideways glance at his rugged profile as he negotiated the city streets.

"I'll have you eating out of the palm of my hand in a week," he returned silkily.

"And if it doesn't quite turn out like that?" she prodded dryly.

"Then I'll have you eating out of my hand in two weeks!" he flung back with a slashing grin.

"The bigger they are . . ." Elissa began warningly.

"The harder they fall?" he finished helpfully, cocking a heavy brow.

"Precisely. And your ego is definitely of the large-scale variety!"

"Well, I'm getting a good start on my goal today, you have to admit. At least you'll be eating my food in my lair. It's only a short step from there to my palm, I'm sure," he purred teasingly.

"Don't count on it," she advised coolly, convinced that if she had anything to say about the matter he would be the one eating out of *her* hand.

"How can I help but be optimistic? See how far our relationship has come since Friday!"

She groaned almost good-naturedly.

"You're impossible. You know that, don't you?" It was going to be a little too easy to get into the spirit of his banter, she thought reluctantly.

"Not impossible, honey, just a bit different from what you're used to dealing with in men. That's my big advantage in this game, you see. I don't mind admitting it."

She shot him a quick, speculative glance. "You call it a game, but you don't really see it that way, do you?" she hazarded with a flash of intuition.

"How do you think I see it?" he asked mildly, slowing for a stoplight and using the small break to trap her glance across the short distance between them.

"More in the nature of open war, I think," she proffered dryly.

"A battle is a battle. Only the stakes involved and the ruthlessness of the day determine whether it slides over the boundary between game and war," he said with sudden soft intensity.

She stared at him in an appalled little silence. "And you're very familiar with war games, aren't you?"

"I've told you, I'm used to fighting for what I want." He shrugged as the light changed and he put the powerful car back in motion with easy expertise.

Elissa swallowed to soothe a dry mouth. She was accustomed to getting what she wanted, too, but not by fighting. Things just happened easily in the normal course of events. . . .

Wade's apartment turned out to be an attractive town house overlooking Lake Washington. Elissa could see the modern West Coast influence in the angled lines of the roof and the wide expanse of glass.

"You were lucky to find this place," she remarked, following him up the path to the front door and glancing back over her shoulder at the vast gray lake.

"I put the whole business in the hands of a real-estate agent. I didn't have any time to scout the market on my own. When the agent suggested this place I took it sight unseen." He pushed open the door, and Elissa stepped into the almost severe interior.

And the first thing which caught her eye was the painting on the far wall. She paused, staring at it in mingled wonder and cold unease. It was a seascape, and in a way it was more alien than the pictures she herself had painted, although the subject was ostensibly a real-world shore-line scene. But it was a seascape of devastating loneliness and power. There was in the bleak fierceness of it something more dangerous and awesome than any element of fantasy Elissa had ever inserted into one of her own works. Yet her first reaction was to cry, of all things! She fought that back with determination, thrusting her hands into the pocket of her jacket and stepping closer to the strangely affecting painting. She was about to say something purposely noncommittal when she realized there was another on the wall to her right. A desert scene this time, but conveying the same raw isolation and grimness as the first.

Abruptly Elissa realized how Wade had known she'd done the unearthly scenes hanging in her own apartment. The part of him which was attracted to these forbidding paintings was able to recognize the part of her she put into her paintings. Wade might not be an artist himself, but she knew at once he had an artist's intuition.

"Unusual," she stated flatly. "They look as if they were painted for you alone." She didn't look at him, concentrating on the seascape. She could feel him standing very still behind her and wondered what he was expecting.

"They were," he agreed neutrally.

"They're good," she said simply, honestly. "Much better than my own work." It was the truth. She knew her own work wouldn't have this impact on a casual observer.

"But you don't like them?" he prompted. His tone remained curiously neutral and he still didn't move.

"Liking doesn't come into it," she said before stopping to think. She bit her lip, hoping he wouldn't pick up on the hasty phrase. But of course that was a futile wish.

"I couldn't agree more," he commented wryly. "Just as liking doesn't come into our own relationship. What do you think of the paintings, Elissa?"

"I find them . . ." She hesitated. "Disturbing."

"Not charming?" There was a hint of humor back in his voice, and she turned to look at him.

"No, not charming." She half smiled, untying her jacket belt.

"Good," he rasped gently, coming forward to take the garment from her hand. "My friend who did them would have been thoroughly insulted if you had reacted to them too comfortably. You knew at once they had been done for me, didn't you?" he went on with a perceptive glance.

"Oh, yes. I knew at once. Did you have them commissioned, Wade?" she asked, looking for a way to steer the conversation aside from the path in which he was trying to take it. When he had removed the jacket from her shoulders she wandered deliberately across the room, noting the masculine restraint in the furnishings of leather and wood.

"Yes," he told her, his eyes following her meandering progress around the living room. "I asked Hal to do the first one on a whim. I'd seen his work from time to time in local galleries and gotten to know him. He told me he'd paint a picture for me but that I might not like it."

"Do you?" Elissa queried.

"The first one suited me." He shrugged. "A few months ago I commissioned him to do another one, the desert scene."

"Which suits you just as well?"

"I think so," he said with a slow, quirking smile. "For some reason, something in me identifies with what's in those paintings. They . . ." He hesitated, looking for the right word. "They satisfy me," he concluded.

Elissa nodded, understanding the statement if not her own reaction to it. She was wondering a little desperately how to get the subject off the lonely, desolate, stark canvases when Wade went on lightly.

"Are you hungry?" he asked, shaking off

the mood and heading toward the kitchen with an unspoken invitation to follow.

"Don't worry, I'll do justice to your food. Nothing like a picnic to bring out one's best appetite. Can I help?" she offered politely, watching with a degree of curiosity which surprised her as he began hauling various items out of the refrigerator. It took Elissa a moment or two to realize she was genuinely looking forward to the small adventure. Telling herself it was only the prospect of ultimate revenge which was attracting her, she moved toward the counter to examine the food being stacked there.

"You can spread the blanket out in front of the hearth," Wade instructed, closing the refrigerator door and reaching for a bottle of wine standing nearby.

"A blanket! On top of the carpet?" Elissa asked in amused surprise.

"What's a picnic without a blanket to eat it on?" He grinned engagingly. "Go ahead, I've got one waiting on the back of that leather recliner. I'll take care of this end of things."

"Are you going to supply ants, too?" Elissa demanded as she obediently headed toward the living room to find the blanket.

"No," he retorted very smoothly, very intently. "My affair with you is a personal and private matter. No one else allowed, not even ants!"

Elissa was glad she was out of sight at that particular moment. Not for anything in the world would she have wanted him to see the red color which she knew was rushing full tilt into her cheeks. To hear him blatantly talk of an affair still bothered her. She was going to have to strive harder to retain a cool composure in this dangerous game.

"But, then," she managed distinctly, although it took considerable effort to achieve the cold warning in her voice, "we don't really have an affair going between us, do we? Only a small case of blackmail!"

She sensed his presence behind her as she studiously bent to spread the colorfully striped Hudson's Bay Company wool blanket in front of the hearth. For the life of her, Elissa couldn't bring herself to turn and face him.

"The blackmail," he drawled very silkily, stalking forward to stand immediately behind her as she slowly, reluctantly, straightened from the small task he had assigned, "is the initial hook I'm using to snag you, little witch."

Elissa stood perfectly still, unable to move as she felt his arms circle around her. She realized he was holding a bottle of wine in one hand and a stemmed glass in the other. The glass was pushed into the fingers of her right hand and, his lips hovering in the vicinity of her ear, he calmly poured the wine.

It was a very neat trap, Elissa thought on a tiny wave of panic. She couldn't move away from the cage of his arms at first because of the sheer tension of the moment. Now she couldn't move or the red wine would be splashed across the chocolate-brown carpet. She stood watching in a kind of blank astonishment as the liquid slowly, inevitably, flowed into the glass.

"But once snagged on the hook, I will immediately begin steps to transfer you to the net. A clever little fish can wriggle off a hook, but a net is a much different proposition, isn't it? A net is impossible to fight. It encloses and binds and traps and allows no freedom at all."

Elissa trembled as he ceased pouring the wine and, with a subtle pressure on her shoulder that she didn't dare resist for fear of sloshing the liquid out of the glass, turned her around to face him.

She met the glinting, purposeful silver in his eyes and forced herself to counter it with deliberate, taunting arrogance, a most unusual attitude for her.

"What will this net of yours be made of,"

she whispered haughtily, "that I will find it so irresistible?"

"Tempting things, dangerous things. Toys for a witch who is more accustomed to orchestrating games than she is to being a participant. I may have to catch you with blackmail, Elissa, but I'll hold you with other kinds of bonds," he promised in a voice of velvet-covered steel.

Chapter 5

A hundred times during the course of the afternoon Elissa told herself she should walk away from the decidedly unreal situation in which she had found herself. But each time some undeniably intrigued and dangerously curious portion of her pushed the common sense aside, assuring her that she could handle the man and the net he was weaving. And always she reminded herself that walking away at this stage would ruin any chance she had for revenge. And besides, she decided with an inner flash of humor, his food was very good.

"I think," she announced languidly at one point, watching the soaring flames of the fire Wade had built, "that this will definitely rank as one of the more exotic picnics in my life." She absently swirled wine in her glass and reached for another cracker spread with paté. Her feet were tucked neatly under her as she sat curled on the blanket, and she felt an almost sensual pleasure in the way the fire drove away the gray gloom of a rainy Sunday afternoon.

"Even though I didn't provide any ants?" Wade quipped, watching with satisfaction as she consumed his food with delicate greed. He was stretched out on his side, propped on his elbow, and he put Elissa very much in mind of a relaxing panther. No, wolf, she told herself, munching the elegant paté. Wade was definitely a wolf.

"I wouldn't want to share these goodies with anyone or anything," she murmured luxuriously. "You keep a much more interesting pantry than I do."

"That's because you do your own cooking." He chuckled, helping himself to the last of the small mound of dark caviar. "Me, I've got to rely on imported tins of fancy stuff to impress my guests."

"Do a lot of this sort of entertaining, do you?" she noted with a mocking, slanting glance.

"Not a very subtly loaded question," he accused easily. "You might as well come straight out and ask about the women in my life as make a comment that pointed."

"I wouldn't think of prying into your personal life," she informed him aloofly, wishing it were the truth. She found herself very badly wanting to know about the other women in his world. The knowledge of her own inquisitiveness was thoroughly annoying and she would not give in to the temptation to press him on the issue.

"I don't see why not," he observed carelessly, although she could hear the laughter in him. "I certainly have no compunction about prying into your privacy."

"Don't tell me you're one of those men who want a detailed description of a woman's past romances!" she tossed back disparagingly.

"No," he assured her, sounding completely honest. "I care nothing about the past. I know you're not carrying the torch for anyone, and that's the only important thing. But I do intend to concern myself very deeply with your present."

"Are you attempting to give me a word of caution?" she teased with a cool little smile. She felt the sudden urge of inner defiance and was bemused by its intensity.

"That's a nice, polite way of saying it, I suppose. A word of caution." He repeated the phrase as if mulling it over for appropriateness. "But I think that comes off as too weak. A clear warning would be a better approximation of what I'm getting at."

"You expect me to steer clear of other men while you're interested in me?" she clarified with great civility even as her blood pounded in response to the challenge. She

121

watched him through her lashes as he examined her in return. There was a tightening of the electrical charge between them.

"Most definitely," he confirmed, taking a thoughtful sip of his wine, his eyes never leaving hers. "I told you on Friday that while I'm circling in your orbit I will be the only one in your inner circle." His mouth twitched, as if a sudden thought had just struck him. "This is probably a new experience for you, isn't it? Having a man tell you that you're no longer free to exercise your spells on other males?"

"I thought you weren't interested in my previous relationships," she countered.

"I'm not, but it might have made things easier for me if you'd learned a healthy respect for the male of the species at some point in your life. Still, if some man had succeeded in teaching the lesson you probably wouldn't be available now for me to instruct. He would have caught you in his own net and I would never have encountered you myself." He smiled, appearing enormously pleased with the workings of fate.

"Perhaps," Elissa suggested with cool daring, "the reason no man has attempted to lay down the law to me before is that he knew he couldn't enforce it."

"Are you now trying to warn me?" he asked gently.

"I would hate to see that lovely ego of yours become unduly bruised," she said just as gently.

"You've already bruised it, honey," he allowed wryly. "Each time during the past month when you ducked out of sight to avoid meeting me or refused one of my carefully held out lures, you inflicted untold damage on it. Damages for which I mean to collect, by the way!"

Elissa said nothing, merely smiling her taunting response. He reached out and removed the glass from her hand, and then, maintaining a grasp on her wrist, he pulled her toward him with just enough unexpected force that she tumbled against his chest, her fingers splaying out to brace her fall.

Before she could do more than summon a frown, he had wrapped his hands in the pelt of her hair and pulled her mouth down to his.

"Umm, you taste good," he growled, his lips moving warmly, tantalizingly, on hers.

"I should," she breathed between his sampling, devouring kisses. "You buy only the best wine."

"One doesn't set about seducing a witch

with inferior weapons," he explained, nibbling his way to a point just behind her ear and back to the corner of her mouth. Tiny shocks followed in the wake of the questing kisses.

Elissa felt the tremor which rippled through her body and wasn't certain if it emanated from him or from her own roughened, heightened senses. She told herself first that she ought to put a stop to the slow, compelling embrace, and then came the consoling, rationalizing thought that the lovemaking was an important part of her plan. How could she hope to charm Wade into asking for marriage if she didn't give him the satisfaction of responding to his kisses?

"Aren't you afraid," she demanded a little breathlessly, "of being caught in your own net?"

His hands tightened, and she felt the smooth, coordinated muscles of his body tense as he moved, pinning her carefully on her back and rolling over so that his chest covered hers.

"Afraid of it!" he mocked, his gray eyes leaping alive with a lambent fire. "I'm looking forward to it with the greatest of pleasure!"

The tasting exploration of her lips made

way for a more demanding hunger which seemed to grow eagerly in him. His kisses ravaged the inside of her mouth, his tongue dueling for excruciating moments with hers, forcing a response her body did not seem loath to give.

As the sensuous intensity of the assault continued Elissa felt herself give ground before it. The man was as overwhelming in his lovemaking as he was in his choice of paintings. In both he expressed himself with bold, masculine power. The impact of her senses was impossible to ignore, and somehow it grew difficult to distinguish between the two vastly different forms of attack.

In the paintings which had been done for him she had been exposed to the bleak isolation of a man who has always fought the world on his own terms. The artist had caught that quality with indisputable sureness. In Wade's arms she experienced the relentless demand for her to meet him on the shores of the wild sea or in the middle of that searing dessert and temper the isolation for a time.

And by answering his fierce demands could she succeed in charming him? In weaving the spells he accused her of being able to cast could she exert some measure of power? The heady thought somehow mingled with the exciting sensation of his hands on her body as Wade began searching out the warmth of her skin.

"No," she whispered achingly as he made short, efficient work of the buttons on her sapphire-blue shirt.

"Yes," he muttered huskily, his mouth on the pulse in her throat. And Elissa knew she didn't have the will yet to stop him. Soon . . . soon . . . Fumblingly she tried to catch his hand and push it gently back from its goal, but he trapped her restless fingers in his and transferred them to the buttons of his own flannel shirt.

"Touch me, little witch," he grated as he left her fingers clinging precariously to the edge of his shirt. "Let me feel your hands on me. Pet your wolf and see what happens!"

The demand was irresistible. Even as she felt her breast swell beneath his cold caress she was obeying his orders and undoing the fastenings on the plaid flannel. She heard her own breath catch in her throat as her shaking fingers found the crisp, curling hairs of his chest and began to thrust through them.

His groan of response was utterly entrancing, Elissa discovered. It made a woman yearn to elicit more evidence of his rising passion. It made her feel reckless and daring. She traced soft circles around the male nipples and sensed his spine arch rigidly in reaction.

"Ah, my sweet Elissa," he breathed as he finished his work on her shirt and eagerly pushed back the material. She closed her eyes as she felt him drinking in the sight of her soft curves. She felt first his hands and then his lips on the hardening tips of her breasts as he disposed impatiently of her lacy bra.

"One way or another I'm going to join you in your fortress, even if I have to make the foundations shake! And you'll welcome me when the time comes, I swear it!"

Elissa was aware of him sliding lower, his hands shaping the curve of her hip as he sowed strings of kisses down to her navel. The almost unbearable excitement arced through her limbs and one knee lifted in reaction.

At once Wade's hand moved to the jean-covered inner part of her thigh, stroking her through the material until both of her legs shifted languidly. He leaned farther over and dropped a heated kiss on the contoured line of her waist precisely where it disappeared into the protection of the denim.

Elissa's fingers groped blindly across the

strong expanse of his chest, probing at the lean, tight skin along his rib cage and seeking the flat stomach beyond.

When he began working his way caressingly back up to her mouth she involuntarily clung more closely, her body demanding more of his warmth and fire. The level of passion was new to her, and the temptation to reach out and leave her mark on his splendid isolation was enthralling in itself.

A self-sufficient male was probably a challenge for any woman, but one who taunted you with that challenge, invited you to change him, was like a drug in one's bloodstream, Elissa decided. And the fact that he was so intent on raiding her own cool, remote tower made her long to try her power on him in a way she had never been tempted to do with other men.

"Tell me," she whispered in a throaty, husky voice as she placed a soft palm on either side of his face and raised his head to look at him, "is it ever lonely being a wolf?"

"Is it ever lonely being a witch?" he returned, not answering her question.

"It hasn't been," she said honestly, watching his flickering eyes for some sign. She wasn't altogether certain what sort of sign she expected to find.

"Perhaps you just haven't been aware of

it," he suggested deeply, holding himself very still above her.

"And you?"

"Perhaps I haven't been aware of it, either."

"It's there in those paintings, I think," she told him and saw the passion in the gray gaze thicken.

"Is it?"

"I think so. It's difficult to be sure, because so much else is there, too," she breathed gently.

"What else?" he invited.

"Remoteness, isolation, aloofness. All those things certainly," she began honestly, working through the puzzle of him in her own mind as she spoke.

"Do you want to find loneliness in me, little witch?" he smiled.

"It might give me some sort of power over you," she admitted, searching his face.

"You already have that," he mocked feelingly. "I would never have set out to force my way into your life if you didn't."

"But it's no good as long as you can see it and control it," she protested wistfully.

"I won't let you use your power to play with me," he agreed steadily. "But that doesn't mean I'm not under its influence."

Elissa smiled with charming menace.

"And I'm not willing to risk myself completely in a relationship I'm not sure I can control, so we are left at an impasse, aren't we?" She waited, sea eyes full of the baiting, goading, daring feelings filling her body.

"I wouldn't say that," he murmured with unruffled assurance, eyes gleaming. "We've already made great strides. Yesterday you wouldn't even admit you wanted to control the men in your life. Here you are today, lying in my arms and telling me you're afraid to risk losing that control."

Elissa took a savage grip on her emotions, which seemed to be in chaos, and smiled brilliantly up at him. She would not let her ultimate goal of revenge slip out of sight, not when he held her like this and told her he could dominate her.

"Thank you," she told him with utmost demureness, her auburn lashes concealing the mix of emotions in her eyes, "for a wonderful picnic. It's time you took me home now."

She felt him stiffen and knew he had counted on much more than a few kisses and tantalizing caresses in front of the fire. The knowledge that she had managed to surprise him with her cool ending to the day gave her added strength.

"The meal is over," he conceded, his

words laced with soft resolution, "but the evening hasn't even begun. Stay with me tonight, Elissa, and together we'll find out whose power is the stronger."

"I'm not ready for a contest of that magnitude," she hedged gracefully. "I need the time we agreed to last night. The time to get to know each other. Surely you didn't expect to win this war so easily?"

"A man can hope." He sighed, reading her firm intention in her eyes and giving way to it.

"Come, now," she charged on a thread of soft laughter. "What wolf wants an easy victory?" The knowledge that she would be the one controlling the ending to the intimate picnic filled Elissa with a sense of power that made her almost lightheaded.

"You don't have an understanding of the species," he retorted, his fingertips playing with the vulnerable line of her throat. "A wolf is interested only in the spoils of victory, not in how the game is played."

Elissa heard and decided to disregard the clear warning. She could handle this man. All she had to do was keep her wits about her. "You must think my job means a great deal to me."

The look of surprise which appeared in his eyes at the mention of what he had called his hook came and went in an instant. It was almost, Elissa thought wonderingly, as if he had temporarily forgotten how she had come to be here in his home, caged in his arms. Had he fooled himself into thinking the afternoon's interlude had removed the memory of the blackmail from her mind? What arrogance!

"Your job," he promised on a determined threat, "isn't going to be the main factor in this skirmish. The challenge between us goes far beyond that level. It was only a useful tool."

"Would you have thought so lightly of it if I were the one threatening your job?"

The gray eyes narrowed. "You wouldn't have done it. Those aren't your kind of tactics. Stick to the weapons you know best, honey. Your witchcraft will be sufficient for your purposes."

"I'm ready to go home," she murmured imperiously. Damn the man for being so sure of himself! There would come a day . . .

"And if I'm not ready to let you?" One near-black brow arched quizzically.

"Then I'll know your word is completely unreliable, won't I?" she tossed back with forced lightness. "You did promise me time. . . ."

"I never said exactly how much time."

There was wary hunger in his eyes, as if he were calculating how far he could push his prey this day.

"Certainly long enough for me to forget the real reason I've even agreed to see you, surely?" Elissa made no effort to keep the taunt out of her cool tone. "Long enough for me to forget a matter of blackmail!"

"You'll forget it by morning if you stay with me tonight," he insisted, the roughly cut lines of his face hardening with conviction.

"I'm not yet ready to take that chance. This is, after all, our first date," she flung back quickly, not caring for the way his hands had tightened on her throat. She mustn't lose her nerve at this point. Feminine instincts and her inborn ability to sense another's needs were functioning well at the moment, and they assured her she was on the right track. If she wanted a proposal of marriage from him, she must play her cards very carefully.

There was a suspenseful hesitation in him, and then Elissa saw the lines at the corners of his hard mouth relax slightly and knew she had won. He was not going to push too hard. Not yet.

Slowly he sat up beside her, the gray eyes never leaving her face as she took advantage of the opportunity to do the same. When she broke the nonverbal contact and lowered her eyes to struggle with the sapphire shirt, he reached over and stilled her hands.

"This time I'll do it."

Patiently, with great precision, he redid the buttons and ran his fingers through her hair, bringing back a semblance of order. Elissa sat unmoving through the small attentions, not understanding the almost erotic pleasure she was deriving from them.

Wade stood at her door half an hour later and waited as she turned around to say goodbye. The drive from his town house had been made largely in silence.

"Thank you for a most interesting picnic, Wade." Her voice prim and her manner too reserved, Elissa faced him from the safety of her own apartment.

He ignored her politeness. "Elissa, I have business at the home office in San Jose at the end of the week. I want you to come down to California with me."

Startled first at the suggestion and then at the ragged note hidden behind the steel in his tone, she stared at him, her astonishment clear.

"That's impossible, Wade! You must know that!"

"Why?" He stood, feet braced a little apart, the suede jacket slung over his shoulder, and defied her to come up with a reasonable excuse. The silvery-gray eyes were fixed on her face with unrelenting demand.

"I should think that's obvious," Elissa snapped, growing rapidly annoyed with his merciless approach. He had promised her time, damn it! Time she meant to use for her own purposes! "For one thing, everyone at work would be bound to find out about it and talk. For another, I'm not about to travel anywhere with you. You'd be certain to construe the action as an invitation. As a sign you'd won!"

"Is that how I'll know, Elissa?" Wade watched her, his gaze softening ever so slightly, as if the thought appealed to him. "Will I know for sure you've surrendered on the day you agree to go away with me?"

"Stop putting words in my mouth!" she grumbled furiously.

"Yes," he agreed with a bleak smile. "I'd rather fill your mouth with kisses, anyway!"

Before she could step back out of the way, he had curled a hand around her neck and pulled her face close for his short, hard kiss.

"Goodbye, Elissa," he told her tersely, surveying her wide-eyed, irate expression. "I'll pick you up for dinner tomorrow night about seven. We can talk about the California trip then."

"What makes you think I'll be meekly waiting for you here tomorrow evening?" she blazed, incensed at his easy assumption.

"Just a hunch." The slow, mocking grin spread across his grim face. "And the promise that if you aren't, I'll make life very miserable for you at work on Tuesday morning."

"You wouldn't dare!"

"Wouldn't I? The only reason I'm going to make an effort to keep our affair a secret for a while is that I thought you'd appreciate the privacy. Personally, I don't care if the whole world knows!"

"You'd embarrass me like that at work?" Elissa choked, knowing that if their private quarrel spilled out into the open she would have no choice but to quit and surrender her hope of revenge. She couldn't bear to have the entire staff thinking the worst of her.

He must have seen the incipient panic in her eyes and guessed that he was pushing too hard, because all at once Wade's voice softened.

"There's no need for me to threaten, is there, Elissa? You'll be here Monday evening, waiting for me. After all, I'm not suggesting anything more than another date, am I? A chance for you to get to know me better?"

Elissa slanted a suspicious glance at him, a small frown creasing her brow. "You won't push too hard about the California trip?"

He lifted one shoulder negligently, eyes lighting with amusement. "Surely it's a man's privilege to try and convince a woman to come away with him. I keep telling you I'm no different from other men, honey."

"Don't take that coaxing, wheedling tone with me," she ordered briskly. "And if you think I'm going to spend tomorrow night listening to you threaten me about what you'll do if I don't go to California with you, you've got another think coming!"

"I swear I won't threaten," he soothed, stroking her cheekbone with the slightly rough edge of his finger. Sensitive fingers, she thought inconsequentially, even if they did seem hard and strong. "I promise to limit my discussion of the subject to rational appeals and the usual male pleading."

"All of which will get you nowhere," she promised with fine hauteur.

"Perhaps. We'll find out tomorrow night, won't we?"

Not waiting for her response, Wade reached for the doorknob and pulled it shut behind him, leaving Elissa to gape angrily at the closed door. For a moment she simply stood there, trying to assimilate the events of the day into some meaningful pattern. A pattern in which she could see whether she was winning or losing.

But it wasn't that simple, she realized, turning away and trailing through the living room, an intense, thoughtful expression on her intelligent features. Try as she might, it was impossible to tell who had won the first skirmish that afternoon. Had she made any progress, or had everything gone in Wade's favor?

Shaking her head fretfully, Elissa came to a halt in front of the crammed bookcase in her bedroom, her eyes automatically searching for the new fantasy novel she had bought during the week, the novel she had originally intended to spend the day reading.

She needed it now, more than ever, she told herself, plucking the exotically illustrated paperback from the stack. Her eyes scanned the cover painting, which depicted another artist's concept of an alien world, and then she kicked off her shoes and settled herself in the middle of the bed with a grateful sigh.

What she needed now was to lose herself in a tale of real magic and sorcery, she realized. For her that reality had always been found between the covers of a book, or else it had flowed from her paintbrush. She was thoroughly at home with the business of retreating into a world of imagination.

But she had never had to retreat from the real world because it bordered on the dangerous, she thought, opening the book to the first chapter. The real world had never been anything other than completely comfortable and totally manageable. It was in such fantasy tales as the one in her hands that her mind found the adventure and magic it craved.

But even as her eyes absorbed the first sentence, Elissa recognized that something was different this time. The book promised to be a good one, full of excitement and the wizardry of a far-off world. So why wasn't she plunging into it with her usual enthusiasm?

Deliberately she forced herself to finish the first page, and then, with a groan of self-disgust, she let the cover close.

Morosely she stared down at the colorful scene of a warrior mounted on a creature that was half dragon, half horse. In the background an evil-eyed sorcerer lifted his hands, frozen by the artist in the act of casting a spell. A good book. She knew it was going to be a good book. And it had started off well, lots of excitement right there on the first page. And she had meant to read it today, anyway.

Damn that man! With a muttered oath, Elissa grimaced down into the unresponsive face of the hero on the book's cover. She knew why she couldn't throw herself into this book tonight. She might as well acknowledge the reason and be done with it.

It was simple enough. The book offered her nothing more exciting than her own real-life adventure. For the first time since she could remember, Elissa had found an adventure that tugged at her emotions and excited her mind as thoroughly as any novel of the far future or the mythical past. Whatever Wade Taggert had intended to achieve today, he had certainly spun his web skillfully.

Elissa lifted her eyes to stare blankly at the painting across the room, her fingernail tapping gently on the slick cover of the paperback book. But instead of her own fantastical work, she saw again the stark isolation in the paintings Wade had commissioned from his friend. A friend who had seen the truth in his patron.

But that isolation was there because Wade wanted it, she told herself forcefully. She had no business feeling a tug of sympathy for a man who certainly wouldn't welcome it. He was a wolf, and wolves were, by nature, lonely creatures. How could creatures who viewed the rest of the world as a battleground ever develop close, meaningful relationships? Wade wanted a woman, and he had singled her out as the chosen victim. He would try to take what he wanted. It was his nature.

And if he could achieve his goal by seduction, that's the weapon he would use, Elissa realized. If he thought threats were the means to his end, he would try them. And if he thought he could use his self-imposed isolation and loneliness to appeal to her gentler nature, he wouldn't hesitate to do so.

She would be a fool to soften toward Wade Taggert in any way. She must remember she was only seeing him so that she could pursue her own goal, that of revenge.

"You think it's going to be easy, don't you, wolf?" Elissa whispered through gritted teeth. "You think you can just make up your mind to have me and that's all there is to it! But I'm on to you. I know what you are. You're a predator, and predators deserve no sympathy whatsoever. And they don't deserve the least amount of kindness!"

No, she was involved in this adventure strictly for her own reasons, not because she was actually attracted to Wade Taggert. such a thing couldn't possibly be! It would be impossible to love a man . . . Elissa's thought broke off in sheer panic. Love! Where in the universe had that idea originated? Of course she wasn't in any danger of falling in love with a wolf! Her imagination really was running away with her tonight!

Grimly she forced herself to reopen the fantasy novel in her lap. She had always been able to control the real world, and Wade Taggert's advent into her life could be controlled as well. It was only in tales like the one in her hands that life genuinely became an adventure.

Chapter 6

"Wise girl" was Wade's dry observation when Elissa opened her door to him Monday evening.

"I assume that remark is in reference to the fact that I decided to go out with you tonight," she muttered coolly. "Let me tell you, Wade, such comments are not calculated to put me in the best of moods for an evening. But you must know that already. Are you deliberately trying to antagonize me?"

"If you must know," he told her, detaching himself from the doorframe and sauntering into her living room, "I half expected you to stand me up tonight." He tossed her a casual, satisfied smile that said volumes.

"That would have been a pity when you took so much effort to dress for the occasion." She raked his expensive charcoal-gray suit and the white shirt with its subtly woven pattern, her eyes derisive. He did look good tonight. Polished, sophisticated, and sure of himself. You almost had to look twice to see the wolf under the surface. But it was there, hidden behind the fine leather shoes and the silk tie. And the wolf in him had fully expected her to be ready and waiting tonight.

"No more effort than you so obviously took," he murmured appreciatively, returning her perusing glance with interest. "You look very lovely, little witch. Turquoise is a perfect color for you."

"Would you like a drink?" Elissa could think of nothing else to say as she endured his open regard. His eyes traveled with possessive approval over the unusual blue, long-sleeved sheath, lingering on the silver at her neck and wrists.

"Have I moved into the ranks of the privileged?" he inquired as she turned her back on him and disappeared into the kitchen.

"What privileged?"

"The men whose drinks you remember."

"Whiskey isn't hard to remember," she tossed back, reaching for the bottle in the cupboard.

"It may be a little thing," he pointed out industriously as she reappeared holding a glass of amber liquid, "but I like to think it's a sign of progress." He took the drink from her hand, glancing at the glass of sherry she was holding for herself.

"If I were you, I wouldn't put too much stock in the fact that I remembered your drink." Elissa smiled with an air of cool mockery, choosing to ignore the sudden pounding in her veins as the gray eyes met hers.

"You mean because such little courtesies come second-naturedly to you? That may be true for your associations with most people, but not with me. I think you remembered my favorite drink because you thought about me last night and today. To us!" he added, clinking his glass lightly against hers and taking a good-sized swallow.

She ignored the toast, frowning slightly. "What makes you think I'd spend so much valuable time thinking about you?" She took a sip of her sherry, striving for a mocking attitude.

"Because I spent the same amount of valuable time thinking of you." He grinned unabashedly. "It wasn't easy, you know, concentrating on my meeting with a new client while wondering if you were going to make me chase you all over town this evening."

So that's why she hadn't seen him at work during the day, Elissa thought. He had been tied up with a new client. She had been lucky. Although Wade had virtually promised not to reveal their relationship at work, she was dreading that first time when she had to react naturally to his presence in front of co-workers. Of course, when had she ever reacted naturally to him?

"Chase me all over town!" Elissa scoffed. "Is that what you would have done?"

"Most assuredly. And the longer I was forced to chase, the more upset I would have been. Which is why I congratulated you on being wise enough to be ready this evening." The look in his eyes was pure satisfied hunter.

"It doesn't bother you that I'm going out with you under duress?"

He looked surprised. "Should it?"

"Some men might be a little bothered by the fact that they had to ensure a date with threats," she growled.

"Some men," he repeated, nodding his dark head thoughtfully. "But not me."

"You don't care how you achieve your goals as long as you get what you want, is that it?" Elissa demanded, setting down her glass of sherry and walking over to the closet for her coat.

She heard him start to say something and then change his mind.

"I really didn't intend to spend the evening bickering with you," he offered ingratiatingly, finishing his whiskey and crossing the room to help her on with the belted white coat.

She flicked a startled glance up at his intent face. "Then we'd better find another topic of conversation, hadn't we?" she managed flippantly.

"How about California?" he asked, sliding his large hands under the wide collar of her coat and holding her still for his brief, hard kiss.

"Another bad choice, I'm afraid," Elissa muttered, acutely aware of the feeling of having just been branded by his lips. She ducked her head and pulled free of his hands. "Where are we going tonight?"

"The Space Needle," he replied readily enough, making no attempt to force the discussion of California on her. He took her arm and opened the door. "Any objections?"

She raised an eyebrow. "Would it matter if I did object?"

"Oh, yes," he assured her deeply. "It would matter. But I don't expect you to do so."

"Why not?" she asked, intrigued in spite of herself.

"It's your kind of building. A revolving restaurant perched on top of the more than five-hundred-foot spire. It looks like something off the cover of one of your fantasy novels." He chuckled as they made their way toward the elevators.

Elissa grimaced, acknowledging the appropriateness of his choice. It occurred to her that, while she had eaten at the Needle on occasion, no one had ever taken her there specifically because it was her kind of building.

City lights gleamed wetly in the Seattle night as Wade drove through the downtown district, underneath the monorail which carried visitors back and forth to Seattle Center, and finally parked near the Needle. They walked through the grounds of the center en route to the glass elevator which would take them over five hundred feet into the air to the restaurant. Wade glanced around with interest, and Elissa smiled.

"The grounds are all left over from the World's Fair held here in the early sixties," she explained. "Seattle has turned the whole thing into a very useful city park and recreation area. There's a science center and rides for the kids and restaurants. Something special going on almost every weekend."

"What else can you do with leftovers from

a World's Fair?" he joked as they joined the crowd getting into the elevator.

Elissa was about to respond when, in the crush of nicely dressed people, she found herself pushed inevitably closer to Wade. Without a word he put out his arm, pulling her against his side with a casual possession. There wasn't much she could say or do in the tightly pressed crowd, and Elissa realized Wade was as fully aware of that as she was.

"Don't worry, honey," he murmured directly into her ear. "I won't let you get trampled."

"I wasn't aware I was in danger," she retorted tersely.

"Um, but you are. A great deal of danger," he countered in a low, seductive tone that brought the red into her cheeks. "But I'll take care of you, never fear."

"I'll bet!"

"I've told you before you're going to have to come to me on faith, little witch," he reminded her.

Before Elissa could think of a suitable rejoinder, the elevator doors slid open, spilling the crowd into the elegant lobby of the restaurant. Wade took over with easy assurance, and without any delay they were guided to a window booth.

"For a stranger in town, you did all right

in securing the best view in Seattle," Elissa had to say as she slipped happily into her seat and instantly turned to study the spectacular revolving scene of the city below.

"The maître d' is a businessman, like maître d's everywhere," he noted laconically, his gray eyes on Elissa's profile as she stared, fascinated, at the view.

"Meaning you tipped him well?" She smiled, glancing around and colliding with his gaze across the candlelit table. It was a small, intimate shock.

"Meaning we came to an amicable arrangement."

"I tried tipping a maître d' once," Elissa confided, her eyes full of laughter at the memory.

"And?" Wade prompted expectantly.

"And he gave me the seat I wanted and then handed me back the money. It was very embarrassing!"

"The poor man probably took one look into those sea-colored eyes of yours and knew he was dealing with a witch. You charmed him into giving you back the tip, didn't you?" Wade chuckled knowingly.

"I most certainly did not! I was trying to practice the proper way of taking a gentleman out to dinner, and having my tip thrust back at me ruined everything," she snapped indignantly, remembering the incident with chagrin.

"Taking a gentleman out to dinner?" he echoed, sounding surprised. "Trying to put the 'new equality' into practice?"

"What's the matter? Don't you approve?" she taunted, pleased at the faintly disgusted expression on his rugged face.

"No!" he stated unequivocally.

"Good!" she said with relish, thinking his words confirmed his basic hunting instinct. A wolf wouldn't like his victim even nominally in charge of the evening, and paying the bill went a long way toward giving one the upper hand. "Just for that, I hope that someday you get a woman boss!"

He gave a crack of laughter — a rich, deep sound that turned an amused head or two at a nearby table. The gray eyes flared more brilliantly than ever. "I've got news for you. I've had one! It was several years ago, and it worked out fine." He looked mildly proud of himself. "And not the reason you're thinking, either," he added smugly when she eyed him skeptically. "I didn't seduce her."

"I wasn't inferring that."

"Yes, you were, and it's totally untrue. We got along fine because she was competent. In the business world that's all I demand of anyone, male or female."

"You're forgetting something," Elissa purred gently. "You also demand that they live up to certain moral standards. I was quite competent."

For the first time since she had known him, Wade looked momentarily uncomfortable, but he recovered immediately. "I do demand a bit more of someone when he or she is being considered for promotion," he clarified smoothly.

"I see," Elissa said stiffly and turned her attention back to the jeweled night outside the window. "Fantastic view, isn't it?" she went on with determined chattiness. "From this perspective you can really see how much Seattle loves the water. The stuff is everywhere! That dark blob over there is Lake Union, and then there's Puget Sound and Elliott Bay and Lake Washington . . ."

"San Francisco has a lovely bay," Wade interposed coolly. "Come down to California with me and we'll spend the weekend there."

Elissa met the waiting gleam in the gray eyes and smiled sweetly. "Not a chance. And you're going to ruin this evening if you continue to bring up the subject."

"It's an important one to me," he protested, contriving to look hurt.

"I'm sure you'll have plenty of company

when you get to California. Lots and lots of old friends to look up," she told him nastily.

"I thought you decided I was a *lone* wolf."

"Not that *lone!*"

Somewhat to her surprise, Wade allowed Elissa to get away with the light banter, not pushing the California trip again during dinner. They dined leisurely and elegantly, with good wine, good food, and Elissa had to admit, good conversation. It was, she reflected at one point, a new experience to be so personally involved in a conversation. Her normal role, the one she chose deliberately, was that of listener or confidante. She couldn't remember ever having had a man ask so many personal questions of her before in her life. The only explanation was that she wasn't really guiding the conversation as she normally did. This one just seemed to flow. She glanced apprehensively at the low level of the wine bottle and wondered if that was a factor.

"When did you start reading those fantasy novels of yours?" Wade demanded as he refilled her glass.

"I don't remember," Elissa replied honestly. "Somewhere in grade school I got involved in science fiction, and when fantasy became such a big part of it I guess I naturally gravitated in that direction."

"Naturally," he mocked gently. "It suits you."

Elissa cocked her head speculatively. "What suits you, Wade?"

"You," he answered unhesitatingly. He smiled his wolf's smile.

"I mean," she retorted firmly, "what sort of hobbies suit you?"

"I don't have any except you."

"I find that hard to believe."

He shrugged uncaringly. "It's the truth. The rest of my life is filled with work."

Elissa frowned. "Work? That's the most important thing in your life?"

"It has been until recently."

"Well, to each his own, I suppose," she remarked slowly, wondering how he classified the women in his life but not quite daring to ask. Perhaps, like herself, they constituted temporary hobbies. She thought again of the paintings in his home and realized that whatever status women held in Wade's world, they didn't manage to penetrate the essential loneliness of it. Because he didn't want them to do so?

"No lectures on the evils of devoting one's whole life to work?" He grinned challengingly, watching the flicker of expression in her eyes.

"Obviously you have a lot of energy to

channel," she replied carefully, perceptively. "It's probably safest to channel it into work. At least, if you bite an employee once too often he or she can quit."

"Is that what you're going to do?" he inquired deliberately, watching her through narrowed eyes, as if assessing how many bites he could take out of her before she fled.

Elissa only smiled, letting him read anything he wanted into the nonverbal reply. She wanted a lot more than the satisfaction of quitting her job.

"I thought," he went on after a moment, "that we would go down to the wharf when we've finished dinner. You can show me around the waterfront."

"If you like," she agreed politely, for the first time beginning to wonder if matters were going to get awkward when it came time to go home. She must make very certain he understood she wanted to be taken back to her own apartment, *not* his place!

But Elissa put the nagging problem out of her mind as she toured the lively Seattle waterfront with him after dinner. It was a bustling, touristy place filled with fascinating import shops, colorful bars, and sea gulls who appeared more interested in eating than sleeping.

She was aware of the contact Wade retained throughout the meandering tour, his large hand folded firmly around her own, and wished the clasp didn't convey overtones of masculine protectiveness. She didn't want to feel protected by this man. For one thing, it would be a false sensation. His protection would last only as long as he was interested in her, and there would be an extremely high price tag attached. She knew that in her bones.

As usual, the import shops proved most attractive to Elissa, and she drew Wade to a halt beside a huge wicker chair.

"I've been thinking of buying that chair for six months," she confided.

He glanced curiously at the fan-shaped back and exotic styling. "Why haven't you?"

"Because, although it looks beautiful, it isn't very comfortable." She sighed morosely.

"And you always put comfortable things in your apartment, do you?" He grinned suddenly.

"Always!" she snapped, goaded by his teasing.

An hour later, chilled from the brisk breeze off the water, Elissa found herself expertly stuffed into the Jaguar and headed for home. Her own home, she realized, relieved that there wasn't going to be an argument over the matter. Perhaps Wade was intuitive enough to know she wouldn't have reacted well to the notion of being taken back to his place. Of course, now she had the decision to make about inviting him in for a nightcap. Why was this revenge business so full of dangerous little pitfalls?

At the door of her apartment she tried turning to make a formal, emphatic good-night, but somehow he was moving into the living room with her and closing the door behind him with a definite finality. Elissa frowned. She might have been of two minds about inviting him in for a drink, but she did not appreciate having the decision made for her.

"Thank you for a lovely evening, Wade," she began carefully as he calmly slipped off his jacket and loosened his tie. "Since we both have to be at work early in the morning, I think we had better —"

"I'm not going to be at work in the morning," he interrupted easily, casting her a mocking glance as he slung his jacket over a chair and stepped close to her. "I'm going to be on my way to California."

"I thought you were going down at the end of the week," she said in surprise, uncertain of his mood.

"I've changed my mind. The only reason for making the trip at the end of the week was so that I could have the weekend there with you. But if you're not going to come with me . . ." He let the sentence trail off invitingly as he lifted a hand and wrapped it gently around her neck.

"I'm not!"

"You're sure, Elissa?" he whispered throatily, bending his dark head to tease her lips with his own.

"I'm sure," she mumbled against his mouth, conscious of the electricity in the air. What would it be like if she were to fling caution to the winds and run off for a weekend with this man? Instantly she squashed the idea. He had insulted her, mocked her, and now he wanted to use her. How could she even think of running off with him? Revenge was what she was after, and she must not let herself be seduced by the charm he could wield. She had to keep her goal firmly in mind, or she would be swept up into the vortex of the passion he could create between them.

"If I asked you very nicely?" he coaxed softly, his mouth tasting hers and then beginning to nibble appreciatively. With his other hand he toyed with the thick pelt of her hair.

"I don't think you know how to ask anything very nicely," Elissa managed to contradict, standing very still beneath his light, intriguing caresses. A dangerous man. Already she could feel the flicker of excitement and warmth beginning to build toward a flame. Her body remembered the way it had luxuriated in his arms on Sunday afternoon and instinctively sought to move closer to him. Desperately she strove to control her reactions.

"You do like to push a man, don't you?" he grated, and then, instead of the delicate little nibbles he had been taking, Wade began to devour her mouth fully. With the eager, hungry forcefulness of the predator, he parted her lips and explored the warm, honeyed place beyond.

"Oh!" Elissa moaned the small sound from deep in her throat, trembling beneath the onslaught and searching wildly for a way of handling herself. Why did it have to be this man who had such an effect on her? If only it were Dean or any of a number of others she knew! It didn't seem fair.

"Come with me, Elissa!" he growled, raising his mouth an inch from her own and meeting her wide, uneasy gaze. "Let's make a weekend of it, honey. It will be perfect."

Elissa felt herself drowning in the silver

159

quicksand of his eyes and struggled desperately to pull back.

"Everyone would know. The people at work would find out about a thing like that, Wade," she protested, clutching at the only straw available.

"I've had second thoughts on the practicality of trying to keep our affair a secret," he admitted, a thread of humor running through the passion in his voice. "I don't think it's going to be possible."

"You wouldn't tell anyone!" she gasped, shocked back to reality at the thought of her co-workers learning of Wade's interest in her.

He hesitated, as if seriously thinking about it.

"Wade!"

"Listen to me, Elissa," he said softly, sounding as if he were trying to reason with her. "Even if neither of us says a word, people are going to realize something's going on. Why shouldn't we be honest about it?"

"Because so far there is no affair, damn it!" she hissed. "So far I am merely studying the possibility, remember? I may decide my career at CompuDesign isn't worth putting up with your attentions." Elissa was angry now — angry at his presumption, angry at how difficult it was going to be to achieve any measure of revenge, and angry at herself for wanting to go to California.

"All right, sweetheart," he soothed. "Take it easy. We'll do it your way."

"You give me your word not to say anything to anyone?" she charged.

"I promise not to make a general announcement," he agreed lightly. "But it's not going to be my fault if someone happens to see us together or notices the way I look at you."

"Oh, yes, it will be your fault. I'll hold you personally accountable if you give anyone the idea that you're interested in me."

"That's a little extreme," he pointed out dryly.

"I happen to feel extreme about it! This whole damn situation is extreme!" she gritted, thinking helplessly that the evening had been quite pleasant up until now. "Blackmail generally is considered *very* extreme, you know! Wade . . . !"

Elissa's railing words were abruptly cut off as he jerked her toward him, pinning her in his arms. She gazed up at him furiously, her sea eyes stormy with the force of her emotions.

"Stop using that word, damn it!" he almost snarled, and then he was crushing her mouth, not seeking her cooperation this time but taking his fill of her. She struggled for a moment and then went rigid as his hand lazily prowled up from the curve of her hip to find her breast. It settled there, branding his possession through the material of her dress and into her skin.

"The next time you're tempted to lose your temper with me, little witch," he cautioned thickly, "remember that not all of us fight magic with magic. Some of us have other techniques." He emphasized the threat by dragging his thumb heavily across the outline of her nipple, sending sparks along Elissa's nerve endings.

"You mean men like you resort to brute force when you can't hold up your end of an argument?" she managed to hiss.

He loosened his grip, retaining only the mildly punishing grasp on her neck, and smiled wickedly.

"Wolves use the most efficient means to end a hunt, darling, didn't you know that? I keep telling you they're interested in the final results, not the game playing that goes before the victory."

Elissa glared at him seethingly, knowing that the excitement racing through her veins was every bit as dangerous as his threats. She would bring this man to his knees for the rude, uncivilized way he was pushing past the dragons and into the privacy of her castle, she promised herself violently. Wade Taggert would pay for his presumption.

"You see me as a victim?" she muttered.

"I see you as a prize," he corrected softly.

"Strangely enough, that doesn't relieve my mind one bit!"

"It isn't supposed to relieve your mind. I'm not out to make life comfortable for you, honey." His momentary anger over her use of the term *blackmail* seemed to have disappeared. Wade was back to the bantering, mocking; seductive man she had known all evening, and Elissa stared at him mistrustfully.

"But you expect me to make life comfortable for you?" she countered vengefully.

"Oh, yes. Eventually. Or, at least, as comfortable as one can be around a witch."

The fingers on the back of her neck moved, giving her the smallest of shakes, as if trying to secure her entire attention for his next words.

"You will behave yourself while I'm gone, won't you?"

"I always behave myself," Elissa announced haughtily, hoping he would take his hand away from her neck before he inflicted damage.

"I'm very glad to hear that." He nodded.

"I would hate to come back to find out you hadn't taken our relationship seriously."

"More warnings, Wade?" She lifted one eyebrow interrogatingly.

"If you need to ask, I'm being too subtle," he muttered gruffly. "Just remember that you're wriggling on my hook and you're headed for my net. I wouldn't take it kindly if you were to allow yourself to be stolen in the middle of the process."

"What? You have so little faith in your own abilities?" Elissa tossed her head, freeing herself from his grasp as she mocked him, daring to laugh at him with her eyes.

"Do us both a favor, honey, and don't push too hard," he advised almost cordially. "Wolves can get awfully short-tempered if sufficiently provoked. I'll see you as soon as I get back from California." He turned and strode away down the hall toward the elevator, not looking back.

Elissa slammed her door as loudly as she dared, instinctively not wanting to disturb the other tenants, and collapsed back against it, reviewing the evening morosely.

Had she accomplished anything at all? There was no doubting Wade's genuine, if temporary, interest in her. The offer of the trip to California had not been made lightly. He had wanted her with him.

But that was a long way from offering marriage, she thought gloomily, straightening slowly and heading dejectedly toward the bedroom. How did one go about maneuvering a wolf into marriage? The problem would have been ludicrously simple with a man like Dean, but with Wade it became far more difficult.

The problem in dealing with Wade, Elissa decided as she slid down the zipper of her dress and slipped the garment over her hips, was that a woman couldn't always be certain who was doing the maneuvering. She might be operating from the relative safety of a castle wall, but Wade had the undeniable advantage of the lone hunter's mentality: a relentless drive that didn't acknowledge defeat easily.

She stopped for a moment and glanced at one of the paintings on the bedroom wall. An alien world full of challenge and mystery. She felt as if she had just finished an evening in such a place.

Chapter 7

It was a relief to be able to go into work the next morning and know she wouldn't run into Wade, Elissa thought. The past few days had been more than a little traumatic, she acknowledged ruefully, and the idea of pretending nothing had happened between them was more than she wished to deal with at that point. Knowing she had two days of grace at the office was enough to enable her to deal with friends and co-workers on an ordinary basis.

It was early afternoon when the phone rang, and she set aside her work on the final draft of a software manual to answer it.

"Dean!" she exclaimed mildly, pleased with his call. "I had no idea it had gotten so late. Where has the day gone?"

"What do you mean, late?" he demanded cheerfully. "It's only a little after one o'clock."

"I know. That's what I mean." She chuckled. "I never get calls from you until after the stock market's closed back east. I worked through lunch and hadn't realized the time. How are things going?"

"Not a bad day," he admitted, sounding pleased with himself.

"Sounds like you pulled off a coup among the bulls and the bears."

"Umm. Why don't I tell you some of the choicer details over dinner tonight?" She could hear the smile in his voice and knew he really was pleased with his accomplishments for the day.

"I'd love it," Elissa heard herself say even as the tiny warning jolt of memory flashed alive in her head. She could see Wade standing in her doorway the previous evening telling her to behave. Coolly, firmly, she pushed the image aside. Whatever Wade Taggert might think, he did not have any genuine control over her life. She was only stringing him along until the moment of revenge, and she would not disrupt her ongoing relationships with others just because of that. "What time?" she demanded, reinforcing her decision.

"I'll pick you up around six. I thought we'd try that new French restaurant downtown."

"A successful day, indeed!" she teased. "That place is expensive."

He laughed. "This is a feast-or-famine business, and today we're feasting."

"Give me the steady salary any day. I like to know where my next meal's coming from, even if I can't always afford to have it at French restaurants," Elissa told him roundly.

"No sense of adventure," he complained good-naturedly.

It was only later, after she'd hung up the phone, that Elissa thought about his words. No sense of adventure. A slow smile tugged at her lips as she went back to the draft of the computer manual. If only people knew how much adventure had recently been injected into her life!

By her normal standards, dinner was a success, Elissa told herself resolutely several hours later as she said her good-night to a smiling and contented Dean Norwood. Smiling and contented even though he was being shown her door after only one short brandy in her living room.

"It was a lovely evening." She smiled dazzlingly. "And congratulations again on the huge block trade today."

"Too bad the market opens so early." He sighed, somehow having come up with the notion that the evening had to be ended prematurely because of his work. He was usually in the office before seven o'clock.

"Stockbrokers should save their socializing for weekends, I guess." Elissa grinned, contriving to look properly reluctant to see him go. It was amazing, she thought, that he was so very easy to manage. Skills she had taken quite for granted before she had met Wade were beginning to appear in a new light. She realized how easily she had kept the evening flowing without allowing the conversation to become too personal. Such a trick wouldn't have been possible with Wade.

"You're probably right." Dean smiled, leaning over to kiss her lightly on the mouth. There was no overwhelming male passion in the caress. It was exactly the sort of goodnight kiss Elissa had wanted from him. "I'll call you sometime next week and we can talk about weekend socializing in more detail, okay?" he asked pleasantly.

"I'll look forward to it," Elissa promised. Very gently she shut the door behind him as he walked down the hall. For a moment she closed her eyes in bemusement, wondering at herself, and then she slowly trailed through the comfortably furnished living room, turning out lights as she went.

Last week she had seriously contemplated engineering a different ending to her next date with Dean Norwood. Yet tonight when the opportunity had arisen she had carefully maintained a distance between them. A distance Dean hadn't even been aware of. It would have been very simple to steer the conversation toward the two of them, Elissa thought with a sigh. It would have been very simple to encourage a far more impassioned good-night embrace from him. But she hadn't done it. And she was honest enough with herself to admit that the reason she hadn't was Wade Taggert.

Not that his warnings alarmed her unduly, she decided, removing the soft green jersey dress. There was no reason to fear the man, and besides, she reminded herself bracingly, there was almost no chance he would ever find out she'd spent the evening with Dean.

But in the course of her recent turbulent association with him Wade had made her aware of something she hadn't worried much about in the past. It wasn't that she had never realized how easily she handled people, she mused, slipping into her nightgown and pulling back the soft satin comforter. It was that she hadn't realized that anything had been missing in the curiously one-sided relationships which tended to develop — relationships she controlled easily.

Elissa lay in the middle of her wide, comfortable bed and gazed around at the brightly patterned green-and-white bedroom. A soft, comfortable bedroom. Exactly like her life. Soft and comfortable. Until Wade Taggert had charged into it. That thought brought her eyes to the paintings hanging beside the mirror. The only things in her bedroom which were not soft and comfortable. Her mouth quirking downward at the corner as she gazed at them, Elissa reached out to turn off the bedside light.

Her hand was on the switch when the phone on the nightstand blared shrilly. Elissa frowned and picked it up, aware that it was almost midnight and that calls this late at night could mean unpleasant news.

"Where the hell have you been?"

Elissa drew in her breath sharply at the shock of Wade's silky aggression. He wasn't in a towering rage, she decided at once. He was cool and controlled and dangerous. But he was nearly a thousand miles away, she reminded herself firmly, and he had no real power over her.

"Out," she retorted bluntly, not bothering with preamble any more than he had.

"I've been calling since seven."

"Why?" she asked with deliberate innocence.

"To see how reckless you really are, of course," he shot back smoothly. "You managed to live up to my worst expectations."

"I assume that's a compliment?"

"Not to your intelligence. Who were you with? Norwood? Is he still there?" The questions came rapid-fire, as if he didn't want to give her time to think up an excuse.

Elissa drew on her reserve of inner control and said quite softly and encouragingly into the phone, "Would you like to speak to him?"

There was a heartbeat of frozen silence, and then Wade was the one taking a deep breath. She could hear the forced sound of it even through the phone lines.

"You don't even know enough to be scared, do you?" he observed with unnatural dryness.

"Well," she hedged, "it's been a good job and I would like to hang on to it —"

"I'm not threatening you with your job, little one," he broke in on a drawl. "Whatever you may think, that's not the only weapon I'm holding over your pretty red head. Now tell me the truth, is Norwood there?"

Elissa heard the command in his voice and decided to give in to it. She was already being bold enough on several fronts, and she didn't want to completely infuriate Wade, she realized. That wouldn't help her plans along. No, she needed to walk a very cautious middle ground here. . . .

"No, he's not here."

"But you did go out with him, didn't you?" he demanded roughly.

"Yes, as a matter of fact, I did. He's a friend of mine, Wade, and I don't intend to give up my friends for you."

"You didn't waste any time asking for the lesson I promised you." He swore softly.

"What lesson?" Elissa's brows drew together in a fierce frown as she eyed the telephone receiver suspiciously.

"I seem to recall telling you I wouldn't tolerate other men in your life while I was in it, and then I went on to say you needed a lesson in developing some respect for the male of the species. You may recall the incident. It only took place Sunday," he chided grimly.

"You *are* threatening me!"

"But not with your job," he told her evenly.

"What, then?" she snapped, irritated, but curious in spite of herself.

"You'll have tonight to worry about it," he said with great gentleness. "And tomorrow, too. I'll be home sometime tomorrow evening. I hope you'll have the courage to be in your apartment when I get there. If you're tempted to spend the evening elsewhere in order to avoid me, you might take into consideration the fact that I'll be twice as annoyed with you if I have to track you down."

"If you think I'm going to sit around and wait for you to arrive just so that you can yell at me, you're out of your mind!" Elissa accused furiously.

"Why don't you spend the time thinking of ways to charm me into a better mood when I get there?" he remarked.

"Would it do any good?" she flung back through clenched teeth.

"It might," he allowed thoughtfully. "Tell you what. Why don't you fix dinner for me and see if that does the trick? I'll be there around seven."

Confused and intrigued by his sudden switch to an almost bantering tone, Elissa hesitated. "Are you telling me I can avoid the lecture if I feed the beast?"

"And pour him his drink the way he likes it, let him put his feet up on your furniture, and ask him all about his hard business trip. It might just work, little witch."

"And if it doesn't?" she couldn't help inquiring.

"As they say," he quoted philosophically,

" 'Into each life a little rain must fall.' The only reason it will seem more like a storm breaking over your head than a light shower is that you're so used to good weather."

Elissa hung up the phone with a small crash.

By six-thirty the following evening she had fully rationalized the work she had put into the meal which simmered temptingly on the stove. She was not in the least afraid of Wade Taggert. Indeed, the whole thing was becoming something of a game, she decided. He had dared her to try to charm him out of his anger, and she had taken up the challenge.

It wasn't that she feared his anger, she thought with an inner smile as she checked the coq au vin. Only that it amused her and fit into her plans to see if he was as vulnerable as other men. This evening would be something in the nature of a test.

She felt a twinge of unsettling anticipation when the bell sounded at seven, but she went toward the door with determination, a glass of whisky in her hand. She had deliberately sought for a homey, soothing image this evening and took a quick glance in the mirror to make certain it had come off properly.

The skirt was a soft border print in tones of gold and brown which swirled lightly around her ankles. She had selected a blouse of liquid gold to go with it, one cut with a deceptively demure neckline. Her hair was brushed to a bouncing shine, and there was a sparkle in the blue-green eyes which owed nothing to makeup. A frilly apron tied around her waist added the final homemaker touch, she thought. How could any man bring himself to yell at a woman dressed like this when she answered the door with his drink ready and his food elegantly prepared? There was a welcoming smile curving her lips when she turned the doorknob.

"Hello, Wade. You're right on time," she murmured sweetly, stepping aside for him to enter. "Do come in, won't you?"

He was still dressed in the business suit he'd undoubtedly worn back from San Jose. The near-black hair was neatly combed, the touches of gray very properly complementing the crisp, conservative whiteness of his shirt. He looked tired, she thought with unexpected surprise, but the gray eyes were as hungry and watchful as ever.

"Good evening, Elissa," he returned politely, raking her slender figure with an intent, interested glance. "Do I take it you're going to try and ease my weary body and uncertain temper, after all?"

"You do look tired," she informed him with a sympathy she couldn't have said was real or false. But it sounded real, she consoled herself, and that was what counted for the moment. "Here, take off your coat and I'll hang it in the closet."

He did as he was bid, shrugging out of the garment and casually loosening his tie with what sounded like a small sigh of relief.

"Was the trip unsuccessful or just tiring?" she asked gently, leading him over to the largest of the comfortable overstuffed chairs and handing him his drink as he settled into it.

There was a fractional pause behind her as Elissa picked up her own drink and returned to take the seat across from him. It occurred to her that Wade was thinking seriously about his response. Had he really come prepared to read her the riot act?

"It was successful, I think," he owned at last, putting his feet on the hassock between them and watching her through mildly narrowed eyes. "At least, Roberts is willing to listen to reason."

Elissa handed him a plate of cheese and crackers, which attracted his attention immediately. "What was it you were trying to reason with him about?" John R. Roberts, she knew, was the head of CompuDesign. The man whose position was said to be going to Wade when the older man retired.

"He'll grant the Seattle office more autonomy in contractual matters as long as I will guarantee the results with my neck." Wade smiled wryly.

"Which you're willing to do?" Elissa sipped her drink idly, her eyes on his tired face.

"Of course," he said flatly, leaning back in the chair and exhaling heavily.

"Somehow that doesn't strike me as terribly reasonable on the esteemed Mr. Roberts's part!" she noted. "Why should you be held personally accountable for the results of what is clearly an experiment!"

"Why shouldn't I be?" He half smiled. "In his shoes, I'd demand the same accountability."

"Yes," Elissa agreed after a moment, thinking of Wade's first month at the Seattle office, "I expect you would. Perhaps that's why the old wolf is grooming you for his job when he retires. He recognizes a fellow traveler!" She grinned teasingly and received a speculative smile in response.

"For a Little Red Riding Hood who's on

rather shaky ground at the moment, you seem in excellent spirits this evening."

"What?" Elissa exclaimed in mock distress. "Is that all the thanks I get for setting the stage exactly as you wished? Stop trying to bare your teeth at me, and tell me more about the trip."

He obliged, relaxing visibly as the whiskey and quiet conversation took effect. For her part, Elissa was privately interested to discover that her responses weren't the casual, automatic ones which came easily to her in similar situations. She succeeded in creating the pleasant atmosphere she wanted, but there was a different element in it than there usually was. With an inner start she finally realized she wasn't playing her role because it was easy or because it was second-nature after so many years. She was enjoying herself on a different basis altogether. There was an underlying warmth and excitement in the give-and-take of the conversation which was vaguely satisfying and stimulating.

"Ready to eat?" she asked half an hour later, rising smoothly to head for the kitchen.

"I'm starving," he confirmed. "But I don't know if I have the energy to get out of this chair!"

"Not necessary," she assured him airily.

"I'll serve the meal in here on the coffee table."

With a few deft arrangements, Elissa transformed the small table into an intimate, beautifully set service for two. Candles flickered, and the china and silver gleamed in their light.

"A man could get used to this," Wade observed some time later, helping himself to more of everything.

Elissa blinked but said nothing. The comment had been a throwaway one, not to be taken too seriously. She was fairly certain Wade hadn't taken it into his head to seek a long-term commitment from her. He was still angling for an affair. Well, she would find a way to push him deeper than that before this business ended.

"You're an excellent cook, Elissa," he continued blithely. "Part of being charming, I imagine."

"Goes with the territory," she affirmed pertly. She poured a little more wine into his glass and splashed the last few drops into her own. "Any complaints?"

"About the food? Absolutely not. Nor about the conversation. I got precisely what I ordered. Do you know how badly I've wanted this invitation?" He fixed her with an inquisitive gray stare.

"Was it an invitation?" She mimicked surprise. "I had the impression it was more in the nature of a command."

"Let's compromise and call it a strong suggestion, shall we?" he offered politely.

She heard the hint of gravel in his voice and smiled very sweetly. "You're the boss."

"So I keep telling myself when I'm around you. But it's been difficult making you understand."

"Has it ever occurred to you," she retorted very carefully, wanting to test the ground before she trod on it, "that I might have been a bit afraid of you?"

"No," he declared without hesitation. "It hasn't." He buttered the last portion if his crusty French roll and slanted a glance across the small table. "Why should you have been afraid of me? At least up until the time I caught on to what was going on between you and Randolph?"

"That was unnecessary," she reproved sadly. "Must you bring that incident into the conversation? I'm trying to forget the whole matter."

"Sorry," he apologized without any sign of repentance. "Go ahead and tell me why you were afraid of me for the past month." He popped the roll into his mouth and chewed reflectively, eyeing her.

"To begin with, you're considerably different from the man whose place you took. You must know that by now," Elissa said calmly, sitting back in the large wing chair and crossing her legs languidly.

"Granted. But every new boss seems a great deal different from the one who went before. Hardly a reason for going out of your way to avoid me."

"You've agreed you're not exactly a household pet," she murmured wryly, her sandaled foot swinging gently as she locked gazes with him.

"And my predecessor was?"

"Definitely. A kind, grandfatherly sort of man. He hired me originally, you know. That was a few years ago, before the Seattle office was large enough to have a separate personnel department. I've always had a soft spot in my heart for Mr. Jensen."

"And he always had a place on your invitation list?"

"Certainly. He *and* his wife," she added a trifle grimly.

"I wasn't about to suggest you had seduced him," Wade told her quietly.

"Thank you." Elissa's voice was cool now. "One never knows with you."

"I sense the sweetness and light going out of this evening," he stated with mild regret.

"Forgive me," she purred instantly, soothingly. "I expect I overreacted. As I was saying, I was accustomed to working for Mr. Jensen —"

"More likely you were accustomed to wrapping him around your little finger." Wade swallowed the last of his wine.

"And then you came on the scene," she persisted, choosing to ignore the interruption. "Stepping on people's toes, reorganizing, issuing directives right and left . . ."

"It's called assuming the reins."

"It's called shaking up the staff," she corrected firmly, lowering her lashes. "With considerable roughness, I might add."

"The bottom line to this endearing little confession being that you thought it was safer to stay out of my way?"

"Something like that," she agreed softly, injecting a certain amount of appeal into her words. She waited expectantly for his understanding.

"Is there any dessert?"

"What?" She frowned in astonishment, lifting her lashes to meet the gleaming gray pools across from her.

"I asked if there was any dessert," he repeated obligingly, an expression of total innocence struggling to look at home on his hard features.

"Yes," she bit out impatiently. "There is a dessert. Cheesecake."

"That sounds delightful," he murmured enthusiastically. "I'll help you clear the table."

"Don't bother," she grumbled, rising to her feet and sweeping up a stack of dishes. With an air of grand disdain she headed for the kitchen. Annoying, irritating, over-bearing man!

She had regained control of her temper by the time she returned to the living room with brandy and cheesecake, and she made a point of smiling very pleasantly.

"So you don't believe you might have made me a trifle, umm, nervous?" she pressed gently, watching him polish off the cheesecake in a few short, efficient moves and hand back the plate for more.

"I'm fully prepared to accept that you found me" — he paused as if searching for the right word — "different. That something about me made you wary." He watched her cut the second slice of cheese-cake and hand it back to him. "That much is obvious. But I don't think you were afraid of me. I doubt if you've ever had anything as uncomfortable as real fear in your life." He sat back in the chair again, taking his time with the second slice of cake.

"I think you're jealous," Elissa said suddenly, reclining across from him, the brandy glass cradled in one hand. She smiled with a kindly, patronizing expression as he looked up. "Not of a man in my life," she hastened to add, seeing the narrowing of the gray eyes. "But of what you perceive as my ability to charm other people. You've said yourself that you've fought for everything you've ever wanted. My way must seem much easier and far less wearing to you. Are you hoping that if I let you hang around me for a time some of the ability will rub off on you?"

"I take it you don't think that's likely." He smiled, showing a hint of white teeth.

"Not the way you're going about it," she returned promptly. Deliberately she sipped from her brandy snifter.

"What would be the correct method of obtaining that goal, supposing I wanted it?"

"You should try imitation, not force. You should practice charming me, not laying down the law." Elissa waited while he appeared to be turning the notion over in his mind.

"There's one problem with that," he decided thoughtfully, setting aside his empty plate.

"What?"

"I think your definition of charm in me

would be my letting you do exactly as you pleased. Which, in turn, would hardly be very pleasant for me. No, you can forget that idea. Jealousy I might feel, but not of your techniques. I'm satisfied with my own way of doing things."

Elissa pounced, catching him up on the small admission he'd dropped. "What would you find yourself jealous about, then?"

"The usual thing," he told her blandly, heating the brandy by cupping the snifter in his palms. "Other men. If you really want to charm me, you'll have to convince me you're capable of being faithful."

"A high price to pay merely to keep one's job." Elissa sighed regretfully, aware of the exhilaration she was experiencing in bantering with him.

"Have you got a better offer at the moment?" he growled, not moving but appearing ready to spring even though he was, to all appearances, fully relaxed in the chair.

"Let's just say I'm working on it," she demurred.

"And so," he declared, "the discussion finally gets around to the main topic of the evening." He settled more deeply into his chair, looking prepared to spend the next several hours there.

Elissa tilted her head appraisingly and lifted an inquiring eyebrow. "What," she asked clearly, calmly, "is that supposed to mean?"

"We are about to go into detail on the subject of you and Norwood and last night, aren't we? Since you brought it up yourself, I figured you were ready to discuss it. Of course, if you'd rather wait a while longer . . ." He let the sentence trail off helpfully, as if trying to be gracious. He waited politely for her to express her wishes. But the gleam in the gray eyes was anything but polite, Elissa decided.

"I have no intention of discussing Dean with you. Or last night, for that matter. We've already discussed it. Besides," she went on, smiling most appealingly, "I've spent the evening following your instructions for charming you. You did imply on the phone that you would refrain from the lecture if I served up the proper amount of hospitality tonight, you know."

"Did I?" He appeared to be recalling his own words, examining them. Then he shook his head decisively. "No, I don't believe I said it would work. I merely said you could *try*."

"I did try," she defended drawlingly. "You have to give me credit for that."

"Yes. An excellent attempt," he agreed approvingly.

"But it's not going to work?" Elissa felt the tiny thrills down her spine as she prepared for the battle to come.

"No," he said smoothly, "it's not going to work. You didn't really think I'd let the whole incident pass, did you? That I'd let you get away with seeing another man the first night I'm out of town?"

"I don't really *think*," she returned evenly, "that there's much you can do about it. You were enormously lucky, in fact, to get dinner!" She couldn't resist taunting him, Elissa realized abruptly. He had claimed to be able to master her, and she now knew a part of her could never have let that claim go unchallenged. No one had ever made such claims before. In the end she was going to have this man on his knees in punishment for his unjustified accusations about her relationship to Martin Randolph. It was only fitting she let him find his own way to failure by giving him enough rope to hang himself.

For a highly charged instant their glances clashed across the short distance between them, and then Wade smiled. A very dangerous sort of smile. But there was nothing overly alarming in his next words.

"Actually, I am a little tired at the moment. And there are other things I'd rather do than yell at you. . . ."

"Such as?" Elissa was ready for a verbal skirmish. Every sense was alert and eager. She could win this argument, she knew. He hadn't a leg to stand on. What right did he have to tell her she couldn't see other men?

"Such as kiss you," he whispered, his deep voice husky as his gaze dropped to her mouth.

Was he going to back down without a fight? she wondered, a little disappointed. On the other hand, Elissa told herself, she wanted to reach her own goal as quickly as possible, didn't she? If Wade was more interested in kissing her than he was in scolding her, she was making great progress.

"You can't," she said very softly, "do both."

"I can't yell at you one moment and kiss you the next? Then guess which activity I'm going to choose." Slowly, deliberately, he set his snifter down on the table beside the chair and uncoiled to his feet.

Elissa watched, her mouth going dry in anticipation, as he paced the single step to her chair and put out a hand to remove the glass from her fingers. Like taking candy from a baby, she decided gleefully. She could make this man want her even more than he wanted to berate her for defying him.

She let him pull her up to stand in front of him, and then he wrapped her arms around his waist and held them there.

"You do deserve something for all your charming efforts tonight," he said very softly, promisingly.

"Something besides being yelled at?" she hazarded provocatively, aware of the feel of his hardness as she was forced gently against him. Head tipped back, lips slightly parted, she watched the very male, very hungry flames melt the gray ice in his eyes.

"Yes," he agreed, his words barley above a whisper and thickening rapidly with desire. "Something besides being yelled at . . ."

His hands still pinning her arms around his waist, Wade took advantage of her tilted chin to feather the side of her throat with his lips. The lightest of touches, it sent a tiny shiver through Elissa. A small voice warned her that she was beginning to respond more and more quickly to Wade's kisses, but she pushed the thought aside. Hadn't she won tonight? Why shouldn't she sample some of the fascinating sensations she was coming to expect in his arms? She could handle the man. . . .

A curious, sensual recklessness urged her to kiss the exposed column of Wade's neck where it disappeared into his loosened collar. She pressed her mouth to the tanned skin and felt his instant response. Her arms around his waist were freed as he shifted to hold her more firmly against him.

"You are a very slender thing for such a formidable witch," he groaned in her ear as his hands slid down the length of her spine to the curve of her hip. "How can you be so little and so dangerous?"

"Am I dangerous?" Elissa murmured, tensing for an instant and then relaxing as he used his strength to arch her closer to his warmth. She began exploring the muscles of his back through the fabric of his white shirt and shivered yet again as first his lips and then his tongue teased her ear.

"Very," he affirmed readily enough. "I doubt if you even know the full extent of your power. You've never had anyone to experiment on with the full range of it."

"Until I met you?" she finished dreamily as his fingers edged lower to cup her hips.

"Until you met me!" He crushed her completely against him, leaving her in no doubt of the rising demands of his body. Elissa felt her knees weaken as the knowledge of the strength of his hunger was forced upon her. The fingers she had been using to stroke his back sought for support instead as she clung to him.

His mouth began moving slowly, teasingly, temptingly along the line of her cheekbone, pausing to drop a kiss at the corner of her eye. She squeezed her lashes more tightly closed in response. When his lips neared hers she moaned unconsciously with a hunger which was rising to match his.

"That's it, little one," he encouraged, letting one hand glide up from her hip to her waist and higher to circle her ribs just below the soft weight of her breast. "Cast your spells, and see if you don't get caught up in them yourself!"

Elissa leaned heavily against him, using him unabashedly for the support she craved as she lifted her arms around his neck. His mouth slid along the remainder of its path and closed firmly, commandingly, over hers with an impact that was like the closing of a door.

"Oh, Wade!" His name was a summons, an order, an imperative that he seemed to understand at once. And just as quickly he responded to it, scooping her into his arms with a small rush of power that left Elissa's head swirling. To still it, she rested her cheek against his shoulder and clung tightly to his neck, aware that he was carrying her through the room and down the short hall to her bedroom.

The light from the hall shafted across the expanse of her bed, and Wade settled her gently in the middle of it. An instant later he was beside her, dropping urgent, biting kisses along every inch of her skin as he exposed it.

Elissa felt the coolness on her flesh as her blouse was pushed aside, and she heard his sigh of satisfaction as she searched for the fastenings of his own garments. Her legs shifted restlessly, and he slid a knee over them, anchoring her in place until he undid her skirt.

She made a small, futile attempt to stop him before he had removed all her clothes, some warning bell sounding belatedly in her passion-fogged mind. But he gently caught her wrists, imprisoning them while he completed the task.

"Are you cold?" he whispered as she shivered beneath his touch. By now she was wearing only the lacy scrap of her bikini underpants, and in the slanting hall light she was almost totally exposed to his sweeping gaze.

"Yes," she breathed, not knowing if it was the coolness of the bedroom or the clamoring of her body's demands which made her seek his warmth. It was all bound up together, she realized vaguely. Only Wade could warm her tonight. Only Wade.

He pulled away for an instant, removing his shirt and tie completely, and then returned to tug her close to his chest. He was still wearing his slacks, she knew, and her fingers went to the buckle of his belt.

"You'll soon be warm enough, little witch," he promised, leaning forward to crush her breasts softly against his chest. The crisp hairs teased at her nipples, exciting the stimulating. "We'll both warm ourselves at the fire we've built between us!"

She had his belt undone now, but when she would have tried to strip the remainder of his clothes from him he caught her hand and brought the trembling fingers to his lips, kissing them lingeringly. Then he placed the hand around his neck, his own fingers searching for her small breasts.

Elissa strained against his touch, clutching fiercely at him as he lowered his head to kiss the valley between her breasts and then sought the tips with his mouth. His hand trailed lower, prowling toward her stomach and then moving on to the promise of her thighs.

With teasing, provoking little forays he inserted his fingers just inside the waistband of her lacy underwear, and Elissa cried out.

"Wade!"

"Tell me, sweetheart," he ordered gently. "Tell me how much you want me!"

"I want you," she gasped, her breath coming quickly between parted lips. "You must know I want you!" She could no longer think properly.

His mouth burned on her skin. "You aren't going to turn away from me tonight the way you did on Sunday?" he prodded.

Elissa tried very hard to remember Sunday and why she had refused him then. Surely the same reasons applied tonight, a thread of common sense tried to say. But she had won tonight! He was here on her terms. He was at her mercy! Wasn't he?

There was something else, she realized dimly. Something more she wanted from Wade Taggert. But she could sense the need in him, was aware of the depths of his desire in every fiber of her being. It was becoming very important to satisfy that desire. More important than anything else she had ever done . . . "No, Wade," she breathed, her heart pounding as he placed the palm of his hand against the sensitive area of her inner thigh. "Not if you want me, too. . . ." She longed to hear him tell her of his need, his desire, and — her pounding heart nearly skipped a beat — of his love. Yes, that's what she wanted to hear him say! And he would say it, she was certain of it. No man could do this to a woman unless he loved her, could he?

"I want you, sweet witch," he vowed heavily, using his nails lightly, flickeringly, on that vulnerable inner thigh in an enticing touch which made Elissa moan. "I want you, and I'm going to take you. Make you mine so completely, so thoroughly, that you'll never look at another man!"

Elissa heard the rough, sensual threat in his voice. It cut through some of the passionate mist he had evoked, reaching the nearly silent part of her brain which had tried to urge common sense on her earlier.

"Wade?" she pleaded questioningly, uncertainly, crowding closer to him in an effort to convince herself that she was wrong, that her tremor of fear was a false alarm.

"After tonight," he vowed, his hands tightening possessively as his mouth nipped her shoulder and then soothed it with his tongue, "after tonight there will be no more games with Norwood or anyone else. No other men, Elissa, my lady witch. Only me!"

She heard the ring of grim male resolve in his voice. Heard it and reacted to it the way she wouldn't have reacted to anything else in that emotional, highly charged moment.

"No!" she managed to get out from a tension-clogged throat. "No!" she said again, louder, more forcefully, as she used every ounce of her nearly banished willpower to call forth resistance from her reluctant body.

"Elissa . . . !" She heard the velvet tearing away from the steel.

"How dare you!" she gritted, finally locating the energy to struggle in earnest, her blue-green eyes on fire with a heat that had nothing to do with fading passion. "How did you dare to think you could come here tonight and . . . and *seduce* me into agreeing to stay away from other men?"

Wade's eyes hardened as he took in the sight of her gathering rage, and he reached for her pushing, punishing little fists before she could find a more vulnerable spot than his chest.

"Calm down, Elissa, before you get hurt!" he ordered harshly.

"Now you're threatening to hurt me!" she flung back, outraged. She would have used her bare feet to kick at him, but he perceived the danger and pinned her ankles with the weight of his leg. Unable to move now, she glared up at him, her anger and scorn flashing from the aroused sea of her eyes.

"You have no scruples at all, do you?" she charged bitterly, her breasts heaving with the force of her fury. "When you can't get what you want by tricking me —"

"I never tricked you. What the hell are you talking about, woman?" he blazed tightly, the cold rain of his eyes drenching her taut features.

"I'm talking about coming here tonight, eating my food, pretending to be . . . to be *charmed* . . ." She was beginning to hate the word but couldn't think of a better one. "And then pretending to . . . to want me . . ."

"That's not exactly a pretense!" he rasped, giving her a small shake.

"The way you did, it is!" she retorted with a snarl.

"I thought I was very honest about that particular aspect of the situation," he grated, and she thought for an agonized instant there was a spark of humor in the gray eyes. "What's so unscrupulous about the way I set about showing you that I want you?"

"You made me think you were . . . you were . . ." Elissa gulped, realizing the direction her words were taking her and trying vainly to find an alternative way to end the sentence.

"That I was what, Elissa?" he demanded

sharply, his fingers bruising her wrists as he waited for her answer. When she could only lick her lower lip in nervous agitation, he finished the sentence for her.

"You thought I was falling completely under your spell, didn't you? That you could control me the way you control the others! But that's not quite the case, little witch. I was charmed enough this evening, but did you really think I'd forget all about last night just because you fed me well and soothed my weary brow?"

"Yes!" she swore, stung. "Yes, I thought that because you made me think that! You tricked me! You were going to . . . to make love to me in the hopes that I'd be so weakened I'd agree to anything you demanded, including giving up my freedom. But it wouldn't have worked, Wade Taggert," she hissed. "Never in a million years!"

"You think not?" he growled, his gray eyes mocking her. "You think that if we'd finished what we started here tonight you wouldn't be eating out of my hand by morning?"

Elissa flushed furiously, acutely alerted to the reality of what he was saying. She wasn't at all certain she could have gone on fighting him if he'd succeeded in making love to her tonight. How could any woman fight a man like this after he'd made her his completely? For the first time she saw the real danger in allowing herself to be seduced by Wade. It would brand her forever his. The realization sent a cold chill down her back.

"We'll never know, will we?" she bit out nastily, "Because you aren't going to finish what was started here!"

"What's the matter, witch? Afraid to find out how powerless you'd be if you surrendered to me?" he taunted dangerously.

"No!" she cried proudly, lying through her teeth. "There's no danger in such a thing because there's no love between us!" And then, with more boldness and sheer courage than she had ever exercised in her life, Elissa added, "I could spend the night with you without risk, Wade — that is, if my pride would allow it! But I can't say the same for Dean Norwood. If he were the one here with me tonight, things might be very different!"

The sudden still silence was colder, more threatening, than an iceberg floating toward her, only the tip of it showing above the surface of the water.

"Don't," he finally grated, the menace in him plain, "try telling me you're in love with Norwood!"

"Why not? He has far more to offer than

you do!" Elissa could hardly believe what she was saying. This wasn't the way she had meant to seek her victory. She shouldn't be precipitating matters like this! It was far too risky, too dangerous. But she couldn't seem to stop herself. It was as if the unreasoning elements of a genuine witch had taken control of her body, pushing her into what she was going to say next.

"What can he possibly offer you that I can't?" Wade demanded with royal disdain for his rival. The gray gaze ravaged her scornfully, daring her to compare him to Dean Norwood. She could feel the outraged wolf in him and wanted to laugh hysterically. Was Wade truly so arrogant, so utterly sure of himself, that he couldn't even conceive of her preferring Dean to him? She would show him, Elissa vowed silently. There were other things a man could offer her besides challenge and a continual assault on her senses.

"I'll tell you what he can offer," she smiled, baiting him. "He can offer marriage!"

Once again the iceberg floated, pressing increasingly cold water ahead of it to announce its arrival. But it was too late, far too late to return to the safety of the shore. . . .

"Marriage." Wade repeated the word as if

tasting it, examining it the way he would a business deal. The enigmatic gray gaze trapped her, wide-eyed and breathless, beneath him. "Is that what you want, lady witch?" he asked slowly, meditatively.

"Yes!" It was too late to back down now, even though she knew she had rushed her fences, that she was probably going to lose any chance at revenge.

He shrugged with massive indifference. "All right. If it will put an end to this game you're playing, I'll marry you. It wasn't exactly the method I had planned on using to keep other men away from you, but I suppose it will be effective enough."

Chapter 8

Elissa was never sure how she managed to drag herself into work on Thursday morning. She cringed at every mirror she happened to pass, keenly aware of the dark circles under her eyes she had tried to cover unobtrusively with makeup. She shuddered as she sat crouched over a cup of tea at her desk, grateful for the privacy of her small supervisor's office. She could not remember ever having had a sleepless night before in her life. Wednesday night would have to go down somewhere in a book of world records.

The dreadfully long hours had not passed in wakefulness because of Wade's presence. Elissa shut her eyes and grimaced wryly as she remembered the calm, utterly cool and collected way he had taken his leave after telling her so casually he would marry her. Her lashes fluttered open again as she instinctively searched for something breakable on her desk. Anything would do, she decided grimly, reaching for a pencil. Even as it snapped obediently in her fingers the memory of how Wade had snapped the yellow pencil during his interview with her on Friday sprang to mind.

Elissa hastily tossed the remains of her victim into the trash can.

"Elissa? Got a minute?" Marie, one of the writers under Elissa's supervision, stuck her pert, closely cropped head around the corner of the office door. She was smiling as she did so, confident of her welcome. Elissa was always welcoming. "I wanted to ask you about this chapter on data entry I'm working on for the manual on the Z100 series machine."

Elissa, with incredible effort, summoned a smile. The very fact that it took an effort was a distinct shock. She was in for another jolt when she realized she didn't want to welcome Marie at that particular moment and assist her with her problem. She wanted to scream for some help with her own problems! But, she admitted honestly to herself, how could anyone help her out of this mess?

"Come on in, Marie," she forced herself to say with a fair imitation of her normal pleasant attitude. "What's the matter?"

"I think we'd better get the programming group to explain in more detail how they've structured the entry screens. It looks like they've put in some protection to prevent obviously numerical fields like dates from accepting alpha characters, but I can't be sure. I don't want to put the instructions in the client's manual unless it's certain."

"Okay, I'll get hold of Rob and Mandy. They're handling the programming for this client, aren't they?" Elissa remarked, trying to get back into a businesslike frame of mind as she glanced through Marie's notes.

"That's right," Marie nodded helpfully.

"We've got to get better coordination between the writers and the programmers," Elissa added with a frown. "These notes they make are so much garbage half the time. We need to be working much closer with that group."

"Perhaps you could talk to Mr. Taggert about it," Marie suggested brightly and then bit her lip. "I guess you'll have to go through Evelyn now, won't you? She's our new department head. . . ."

"Yes," Elissa agreed fervently, exceedingly grateful that she wouldn't have to go directly to Wade over the matter. "I'll mention it immediately to Evelyn." She shook her head absently. The interdepartmental lack of communication was one of the things she had planned to devote a great deal of time to improving once she'd been given the new, higher-level position. She would have to work through Evelyn now. Elissa stifled a sigh.

After a bit more professional discussion of the task at hand, Marie left, leaving her supervisor to her private thoughts. And said thoughts returned at once to Wade's incomprehensible leavetaking the night before. Elissa still couldn't understand it, although she had gone over the scene a thousand times during the night, searching for a clue. She had been prepared to tell him flatly what he could do with his proposal the moment she had gotten it.

But she hadn't expected to get it so soon and not under such conditions. The small revenge to be derived from the scene in her bedroom hadn't been what she was after at all. She wasn't even sure Wade would care one way or the other if she threw the offer of marriage back in his face. He was simply extending the proposal because she'd more or less implied his competition was prepared to do so. She'd pushed him into it. He hadn't come crawling on his hands and knees begging her to marry him! Some revenge!

Elissa got to her feet and paced the limited area in front of her desk, her forehead tense with her whirling thoughts. There was one interesting option open to her, she decided after a moment. She could continue with the farce of an engagement, hoping to wring more satisfaction from the situation. Wade did want her, she told herself, even though he'd made no effort to consolidate his position last night. Not that she would have allowed him to do so, Elissa added regally. But he hadn't even given her the chance to refuse him. He'd simply rolled off the bed, tossed on his shirt, told her he'd see her at work, and left.

She gritted her teeth in a grin that would have appeared astoundingly savage if she'd seen her face in a mirror.

Fortunately, running into Wade at work was not that common for someone on her level. She might conceivably have to pass him in a hall, but she would do her best to stay clear of the executive suite of offices where that sort of encounter was most likely. She needed time to think. She *must* think!

But fate was definitely against her, Elissa decided at lunchtime as she made her way quickly down the hall toward the exit. She was rounding the corner, preparing to grab the slowly closing doors of one of the elevators, when she saw Wade at the other end of the hall. He glanced up from scanning the front page of the business journal he had in his hand and saw her at the same time. He was already walking in her direction, and on seeing her he increased his pace.

Elissa thought of how he had accused her of ducking around corners in order to avoid running into him in the past. She took a deep breath. He was just going to have to add another instance to his list of times she had deliberately avoided him, she thought forcefully, stepping into the elevator and letting it close. There was a certain satisfaction to be had from the annoyance in the gray gaze which watched in grim frustration as she made good her escape.

Confident she'd gained sufficient time to allow her to disappear into the noonday crowd on the Seattle street, Elissa stepped out of the elevator a few minutes later and into the building lobby. The guard at the reception desk was in the act of replacing his telephone receiver when he glanced up and saw her.

"Oh, Miss Sheldon," he called cheerfully.

"What is it, Russ?" Elissa said politely, wanting to be on her way out but not wanting to offend this friendly older man who greeted her so cheerfully each morning.

"Wanted to show you those pictures of the grandkids I told you about last week. Finally got them back from the developer this morning."

"Could I see them after lunch, Russ?" Elissa pleaded desperately, conscious of being vulnerable as long as she stood in the lobby. "I've got to dash. Some errands to run on my lunch hour. You know how it is . . ." She was already halfway toward the revolving doors when Wade's voice called her name and she knew she'd lost the small race.

"Elissa!"

She turned in resignation, hearing the iron command vibrating under the assumed friendliness of his call. He was stepping out of the other elevator, moving toward her.

"Thanks, Russ," he threw over his shoulder as he walked past the smiling guard.

"No problem, Mr. Taggert," Russ beamed, his bushy white brows lifting as he regarded the other two. "Always glad to help."

"On your way to lunch, Elissa?" Wade inquired blandly, slipping his hand firmly under her arm. His eyes glittered down at the coolly composed face.

"Yes, as a matter of fact, I was." There was little else she could do except submit to his unrelenting lead as he started her out the door.

"How convenient. So am I. I was on my

way down to your office to invite you along when I saw you stepping into the elevator. Too bad you weren't able to hold the doors open for me, but these modern elevators do shut quickly, don't they? Lucky I was able to use the phone in the other one to call Russ and tell him to detain you."

"The elevator phones are only for emergencies," she snapped, irked at her failure.

"This was an emergency, I think," he drawled. "As I said, lucky I was able to get hold of Russ."

Elissa shot a suspicious sideways glance up at his too-bland face. He returned it with gleaming malice in his eyes. "I'm assuming, of course, that the elevator's shutting and not reopening was an accident. I wouldn't want to think you'd gone back to your old trick of ducking out of sight whenever you happened to come across me in the hall."

"Wouldn't think of it," she told him airily, refusing to be intimidated.

"Good." He nodded. "Now, then, about lunch . . ."

"I was only going to grab a quick bite at the deli down the street," she said bluntly.

"I'll join you." He smiled. "As soon as we pick out the ring."

Elissa froze, coming to a full stop in the middle of the sidewalk and swinging around to glare up at him. "What ring?" she asked very distinctly.

"Your engagement ring. What ring did you think I meant?" he retorted mildly. "There's a good jeweler in the next block. He's expecting us."

"But how could he? I mean, we only decided last night! That is . . ." Elissa broke off in a morass of confusion as she contemplated the new development.

"I called him an hour ago. That's why I was on my way down the hall to fetch you," he explained kindly. "I was under the impression I had plenty of time." He glanced pointedly at the thin gold watch on his wrist. "Most of the staff go to lunch from twelve to one."

Elissa flushed, aware that it was not yet twelve. "I, er, had some chores and thought I'd take a couple of extra minutes . . ."

"So you ducked out fifteen minutes early?" He made a small clucking sound of disapproval. "Not a good example to set for the rest of the staff, is it? You do still have people reporting to you, even if you aren't the new head of editing and graphics!"

"It won't happen again!" Elissa lifted her chin haughtily. "I was feeling somewhat pressured this morning."

"Were you? I wonder why. . . ."

"Stop teasing me, Wade!" she snapped, goaded. Whirling, she started up the sidewalk again, jamming her hands into the front pockets of her belted wool coat. Instantly he fell into step beside her, pacing along like the wolf he was.

"What gave you the idea I was teasing, Elissa? I'm going to put a stop to this furtiveness of yours if it's the last thing I do! Hard on my ego, you see," he explained laconically.

"I doubt if anything could demolish your ego!" Except when I tell you I wouldn't marry you if you were the last wolf on earth, she added silently.

"If you keep talking like that I might get the idea you're a tad reluctant to marry me," he observed coolly. A little too coldly.

Elissa went on the alert. She didn't want to ruin matters at this delicate stage. Not when the situation had begun to promise some interesting possibilities in the way of revenge.

"It was a bit sudden," she murmured wryly, not certain how to pursue her new course of action but committed to it. It seemed easiest to follow Wade's lead for the moment. After all, she would always be able to bring everything to a screeching halt when she was ready to make her grand refusal. That thought gave her a small lift.

"I was only meeting your terms, honey," he purred. "You made it clear the competition was offering marriage: That's a tough offer to beat with only the promise of an affair and a little assistance in your career. I upped the ante in order to stay in the game. I think I mentioned in the beginning — was it only last Friday? — that I'd use whatever lures would work. The way I figure it, I'm holding all the aces again. With marriage thrown into the pot along with good career potential, how can you resist?"

Elissa flicked a half curious, half enraged glance at him out of the corner of her eye and surprised a strangely watchful expression on his features. Something tight in the lines of his mouth . . .

"You really believe I'm quite mercenary at heart, don't you?" she muttered, unwilling to admit to herself that the evidence of tension in him had disturbed her. "Have you given any thought to what's going to happen when you lose interest in me and my career? You did say originally you didn't know how long you'd want me!"

"We'll burn that bridge when we come to it," he promised, pulling her to a stop in front of a jeweler's door. "First things first, however. . . ."

The selection of the ring didn't turn into a

major event for the simple reason that Elissa refused to become overly involved. She scanned the first tray of rings presented her and randomly picked the least gaudy one, declaring herself satisfied.

"We'll take that one," Wade instructed the helpful, hovering jeweler, and Elissa ground her teeth in disgust as her new fiancé indicated a different ring from the one she had selected. It was easier not to argue. Besides, she would only be giving it back shortly, anyway. Throwing it back, perhaps, if she managed things with a proper amount of drama.

"About announcing our engagement to the rest of the staff," Wade began some time later as he pulled off the small coup of finding a table at the overcrowded little deli much favored by office workers in the vicinity.

Elissa glanced up, startled. "I . . . I hadn't thought about that," she admitted slowly, turning this new wrinkle over in her mind as she took her seat.

"Well, you'd better. A well-handled, discreet little affair might have been something we could have kept out of the limelight, but an engagement is more complex, I'm afraid."

"You sound very knowledgeable on the

subject," she retorted, gradually regaining some of her normal poise. She'd allowed herself to become dizzy with the rush of events, but she could deal with them, she reminded herself.

"Common sense," he returned smoothly. "I didn't get where I am by not being able to do good contingency planning."

"Too bad I wasn't more versed in contingency planning myself," she grumbled with great depth of feeling as she glanced through the menu.

There was a split second's hesitation before Wade's reply. "You mean if you had been you might have approached the right man at the start of your campaign for the promotion? Well, live and learn. You're headed in the right direction now. What are you going to have for lunch?"

She told him, and he gave the orders to the waitress, who bustled off in the direction of the kitchen. Wade turned his attention immediately back to Elissa, who waited warily.

"Returning to the matter of our announcement to the staff," he began again firmly. "I think the most appropriate way would be a casual cocktail party at my place. I haven't done any entertaining to speak of since I took over CompuDesign, and this should provide a good excuse." He nodded, apparently pleased with his plans. "We'll make a little announcement sometime during the middle of things when everyone is on his or her second drink, and I'll present you with the ring. It should go over very nicely."

Elissa thought briefly of her engagement ring, which had been left at the jeweler's for sizing. Then she thought of receiving it in front of the entire staff of CompuDesign. Her mouth went quite dry.

"Perhaps we should be quieter about the whole matter," she tried tentatively. That was instinct speaking, though, she told herself bracingly. *Practically* speaking, this might be just the event she was looking for. . . .

"Nonsense," Wade said dismissingly, smiling with an intimidating show of his good white teeth. "The staff will love it. Possibly enough to make them forgive me for choosing Evelyn over you for that promotion!" He tacked on the last statement with a wryness that caused Elissa to lift an interrogating eyebrow.

"Has anyone said anything along those lines?" she demanded in surprise.

"Not directly." He grimaced ruefully. "But I've gotten the message."

Elissa frowned, "I hope it's not going to make life difficult for Evelyn."

"Our announcement should go a long way toward taking everyone's mind off the subject," he pointed out.

Elissa nodded, thinking about the positive effects the action would have for Evelyn, and then her mouth tightened as she reminded herself that Evelyn was not her primary consideration at the moment. The party was going to be used for the benefit of one Elissa Sheldon, damn it!

"I think I'll schedule the cocktail party for Sunday afternoon, say between five and seven. Most people are free Sunday afternoons, and as this is such short notice, that's an important factor. . . ."

"*This* Sunday afternoon?" Elissa blinked her astonishment.

"Why not?" he said carelessly as their sandwiches were presented by the waitress. He thanked the woman with a smile which she didn't seem to find wolflike at all.

"But . . . so soon?" Elissa wasn't sure why the short time frame was upsetting her. Didn't she want to get the whole thing over with?

"What's the point of waiting? Can't you get things organized by then? You always seem quite efficient."

"Me! I'm supposed to organize the engagement party?" Elissa squeaked. Things were getting rushed again, and she wasn't sure she liked it.

"I'll handle the food," he assured her quickly. "Don't look so annoyed; you'll have the easy part. My God! You're glaring at me as if I'd just told you or organize your own execution!"

Elissa drew in her breath at the analogy. An execution, she thought harshly, was exactly what the party would be. An execution of the overinflated, overbearing, and vastly annoying ego of a wolf!

"I'll see what I can do," she promised sweetly, unaware of the gemlike glitter in her eyes.

Wade nodded, looking much too satisfied. "Yes, I thought you'd agree," he murmured softly. He took a huge bite of his sandwich. "When you've finished your lunch we'll take care of another detail."

"Which is?" she demanded tartly.

"The license."

That afternoon Elissa pulled out the old résumé every serious career person is supposed to keep tucked away and began the task of updating it. Whatever happened Sunday afternoon, she would be job hunting Monday morning.

It was strange, she thought gloomily, scanning the one-page summary of her entire working experience, how attached she'd gotten to CompuDesign. She would be sorry to leave. Not *overly* sorry, she realized truthfully, but mildly sorry. Elissa bit her lip and considered that for a while. When was the last occasion when she had been *very* sorry about anything? She shook her head. The only event she could work up strong emotions over lately was the explosion of Wade Taggert into her life. She began to look forward to Sunday afternoon.

She wasn't quite sure what gave her the notion of dragging out her acrylic paints and brushes that evening. The urge to paint had popped into her head after she'd eaten a quiet, solitary dinner in front of the evening news, and she didn't fight it. When she felt like painting, there was nothing else to do but obey the summons. Nothing else would be satisfactory at that particular moment, as she knew from experience.

Carefully she spread a sheet to protect the rug, set out the paints on the palette, and erected a small canvas. Before beginning she went over to the stereo and, after a moment's close thought, put on Bach's Brandenburg Concertos. A little lilting pizzazz was called for, she decided, turning the volume up higher than usual. She bit her lip as the rich strains filled the apartment. Neighbors, she reminded herself guiltily, and reached for the earphones.

Much better, she told herself, the long cord to the earphones dragging behind her as she headed back toward her canvas. The music now filled her head, not the apartment, and picking up a brush, Elissa began creating another world.

It was like a drug, this business of projecting herself into the landscape of a planet circling under a different star. The music swirled in her mind, somehow getting mixed up with the paint on her brush, and except for having to change the record occasionally, Elissa lost all track of time. She forgot about everything except the adventure taking place under her fingertips, an adventure in which magic too, the place of science and strange beings conversed on subjects which had nothing to do with computers or cocktail parties.

She wasn't sure how long the doorbell had been sounding before it finally penetrated the earphones. For a moment longer she hesitated, hoping against hope that whoever was outside her door would give up and go away, leaving her to the painting and music. But it was not to be. The bell chimed again, imperiously, and with a sigh Elissa went to answer it.

The shock of finding Wade on the other side of the door caused her to freeze, brush in hand, as she opened it. A strange disorientation persisted which she couldn't quite comprehend. Her mind was still partially in her landscape, she thought vaguely. She stood staring up at him, saw his lips move, and realized she couldn't understand what he was saying.

The brush waved distractedly through the air as she shook her head, scowling, and then he smiled, put out both of his large hands, and removed the headphones.

"I said, good evening, Elissa." He grinned, holding the source of her music in his fingers. Instantly silence descended, and Elissa found herself emerging back into the real world.

"Hello, Wade," she managed, shifting with a twinge of uncertainty. "What are you doing here?"

"Why shouldn't I be at the home of my bride-to-be?" he quipped, leaning down to plant a rather husbandly kiss on her forehead. He stepped inside and closed the door firmly behind him. Elissa backed up, not having much option, and her eyes narrowed.

"Don't point that thing at me." He laughed, indicating the brush in her hand. "I come in peace!" He held out a palm in the traditional gesture, and Elissa smiled in spite of herself.

"I suppose you've come to plan your grand party." She grimaced, glancing down at her paint-stained jeans and blue cotton work shirt. "As you can see, I've had other things on my mind."

He was dressed casually himself, although his jeans weren't spattered with paint and the maroon sweater he had on under the fleece-lined jacket looked expensive.

"No problem." He chuckled, shrugging out of the jacket and tossing it unconcernedly over the back of a chair. Immediately he made for the canvas across the room, and Elissa grew unaccountably nervous. "I've always wondered what you'd be like caught up in the middle of one of your painting binges," he said reflectively, coming to a halt in front of the scene created out of paint.

"Wade, that's not finished yet, and I . . ." Elissa felt her unease increase and begin to crystallize until she was abruptly aware that she didn't want him looking at the painting. Normally it didn't matter if others saw her work. They never understood it, and it made no difference. But this man was too perceptive, and Elissa realized she was vulnerable in this, her most private area.

There was a tension-fraught silence as he studied the painting with an intentness that bothered her. She was standing on the other side of the canvas, unable to view it, so her mind recreated the scene for her. The memory of what she had done made her wet her lips in anxiety. Surely he would not, could not, see what she had quite unconsciously put into the landscape.

But when he looked up, the gray gaze meshing with hers over the top of the canvas, Elissa knew he had, indeed, seen far too much.

"Elissa, Elissa, my sweet witch," he growled with a beguiling roughness that did nothing to disguise the hint of wolfish triumph in him. "Are you trying to tell yourself something? Or are you trying to communicate with me?"

"I don't have the vaguest idea of what you're talking about," she hissed, moving forward to turn the easel with its too-revealing painting toward the wall. "Come and sit down. I'll get you a brandy. I assume you've had dinner?"

"Good old Elissa, using her charming-hostess qualities to try and take my mind off what I just saw." Wade obediently took the large chair she indicated and made no effort to prevent her from hiding the painting. "But I'm not as easily deflected as that, little one. I would have thought you'd realized that by now."

"Stop talking nonsense," she ordered, hurrying into the kitchen to find the bottle of brandy and a snifter. "It's merely another one of my weird paintings, and you're only fooling yourself if you try reading too much into it."

"I want it for a wedding gift, Elissa," he told her bluntly as she reappeared, glass in hand.

She stopped for a second, appalled. "What?"

"You heard me," he repeated gently, his eyes glowing with gray flames. "I want that painting for my wedding gift. It's traditional, isn't it? For the bride and groom to exchange gifts?" One black brow lifted quizzically.

"Why?" Elissa forced herself to continue her forward progress, carrying the brandy carefully to his side and putting it on the small table near the chair. She didn't look at him as she busied herself with the task. She was able to avoid his eyes completely, in fact, until after she'd seated herself in the chair across from him. Then it became quite impossible.

"Because," he told her calmly, "when it's done it's going to be my invitation into the witch's castle."

"You think so?" she couldn't resist taunting. "What makes you believe you're the one being invited?"

"Don't play that particular game with me, Elissa," he grated, eyes narrowing with warning. "It's the one tactic I won't let you use. I thought we had that understanding clear last night when I asked you to marry me!"

"That I'm not to imply the existence of other men?" she confirmed, an unholy sense of mischief rising inside her as she sought for some defense against what he had seen in her painting. "Very well, I suppose it's only civil if I keep my other interests out of your sight. After all, as my husband I accept you're entitled to some small consideration . . . Wade!"

His name came out on a tiny shriek as he pounced. He was out of his chair and hauling her up beside him before she even had time to comprehend what was happening.

"What do you think you're doing?" she gasped furiously, her shoulders bruising under the hard clasp of his fingers. She gazed up at him in a strange fury. Strange because it was tempered with sheer, unadulterated fear. Elissa discovered that she did not like being afraid. It was a highly uncomfortable sensation, one which sent tremors through her limbs to the tips of her fingers and the ends of her toes. It made her heart pound and her breath quicken painfully.

"I should think what I'm doing is obvious, even to an independent, irritating, willful little witch who hasn't got the sense to know when she's gone much too far out of line," he rapped out in a voice that seemed to roar at her even though he never raised it. The gray eyes swirled with a freezing storm that threatened to turn her into easily shattered ice.

"I am going to beat you, Elissa Sheldon. Another new experience for you, I'll bet. I'd stake a lot of money on the idea that no one's ever even thought of doing such a thing to sweet, charming Elissa!"

"Wade!" Elissa's mouth fell open in utter shock. "You wouldn't dare!"

"There you go again, mixing me up with the other men in your life who fit so easily around your little finger," he mocked, giving her a slight but violent shake. "Perhaps when I've finished you'll be able to re-member which one I am!"

"Wade! Please don't!" Elissa resorted to primitive feminine instinct. Enraged males were to be placated, appeased. It was the weaker female's only defense when matters had gone this far. "Please don't hurt me," she begged, disgusted with her pleading but not so disgusted as to continue the defiance. Discretion was called for here, she told herself grimly. "I was only baiting you because I was upset that you'd seen the painting. You can have it, Wade, I promise," she added quickly, not noticing any signs of the lightning in his eyes abating. She waited, the trembling in her slender figure not in the least faked for the sake of authenticity.

"When I arrived at your door this evening," he told her gruffly, eyes still very hard and metallic, "I was in a good mood. I want to be restored to that mood."

Elissa felt hope flare amid the nervous wreckage of her poor stomach.

"Isn't there . . ." She moistened her lips and tried again, eyes wide and pleading. "Isn't there anything besides beating me that will restore your better mood?" With all the female power inborn in a woman, she loaded the delicate question with soft promise and soothing appeal.

"One hell of an abject apology from you might do the trick," he growled unhelpfully. "The sight of Elissa Sheldon groveling is about the only thing that will have any impact on my recent decision!"

"I'm sorry, Wade," she murmured, lowering her head dejectedly and letting her lashes flutter gently on her cheeks. Pride didn't come into the matter just then, she told herself morosely. She would worry about that wounded pride after she'd gotten herself off the hook. "It was only that I was upset. . . ."

There was a tense, dangerous pause, and Elissa waited in an agony of suspense to see which way his mood would swing. She clutched her hands, palms damp, in front of her, keeping her gaze on the rug at her feet. When this fiasco was over, she swore silently, she was going to look forward to Sunday evening with immeasurably increased enthusiasm. Wade Taggert had a great deal to pay for, and she was going to extract that payment. Every ounce of it!

"No more arguments about the painting?" he challenged with a certain ferocity. "You'll give it to me as a wedding gift?"

She nodded, head still bent. "Yes, Wade." She wanted to cross her fingers as she uttered the false promise but didn't quite dare.

"And there will be no more taunting me with hints of other men still flitting to and fro in your life?" he persisted vengefully.

"No, Wade."

Again a pause. Elissa swallowed with difficulty.

"Congratulations, Elissa," he suddenly drawled, the velvet in his voice not fooling her for a minute. "I do believe you've learned a new spell tonight. One you've probably never had occasion to use in the past, but you might find it quite useful in the future. The thing to keep in mind is that it might not always work on me. You got lucky this time, however. I accept your apology. Now sit down and we'll go over the details of the party. I'll want to order the food and drink as soon as possible."

Elissa stirred, stepping carefully back out of reach. He let her go. She met his eyes, and her own slitted in sudden suspicion.

"You're rather quick to change your moods," she observed dryly, studying him with her head tipped to one side. The storm in the gray gaze was gone as if it had never been.

"Your apology was very nicely delivered," he said by way of explanation, settling back into his chair with a sigh of contentment. He closed his eyes.

"I tricked you," he agreed, not opening his eyes. He appeared the picture of contentment.

"You wouldn't have beaten me." It was a statement, uttered with a certain seething violence. She flung herself down into her own chair, propping her feet on the hassock and leaning back with a sensation of complete self-disgust.

"Not for a little wolf baiting."

"What were you doing? Practicing witch baiting?" she gritted, wishing he would open his eyes so he could get the full effect of the angry flags flying in her own.

"Perhaps," he said enigmatically. "It's a bit more complicated than that, though. I'll explain it to you on our wedding night." He lifted his lashes at last, and the grey eyes actually shimmered as they caressed her sprawled figure. "Now, about that party . . ."

"Speaking of our wedding," Elissa whispered glumly.

"Oh, yes. I forgot to mention I'd set the date, didn't I? It's Monday."

Chapter 9

It was midway through Friday that Elissa finally remembered Dean Norwood. With a small start she glanced up from her work and frowned absently at the far wall of her office. What was she going to do about Dean?

Not that she had any desire to continue her association with him, regardless of her impending freedom from Wade. No, the lukewarm relationship was best ended, and the sooner the better. But there was no reason it couldn't be handled gently and comfortably for all concerned. Dean had been a most pleasant escort, and Elissa automatically searched for an appropriate way of slipping him out of her life.

When Marie knocked politely on the doorframe to announce her presence, Elissa smiled with more enthusiasm than usual. The answer to her small dilemma was suddenly obvious.

"Come in, Marie."

"Hi, Elissa, just wanted to check and see if

you'd heard from Rob and Mandy about those entry screens."

"Yes, as a matter of fact, I did. They'll have the data for you this afternoon."

"Good. I'll be able to complete the manual on Monday, then." Marie nodded, pleased.

"That will be fine. Say, Marie!" — Elissa smiled dazzlingly — "would you like to have a drink with me tonight after work? There's someone I'd like you to meet. . . ."

Marie's warm brown eyes brightened for a moment and then assumed a slightly cautious expression. Her attractive features shaped themselves into a tentative smile.

"You know I'm a bit rusty at social situations these days," she said diffidently.

"You're not going to get over John's defection until you start dating other people, Marie. You know that," Elissa advised gently. Elissa had been the one Marie had turned to for a confidante when her boyfriend had casually announced his engagement to another woman. But that had taken place two months ago, and it was time Marie improved her social life.

"I know," Marie admitted. "Guess I'm just feeling scared."

"You won't around my friend," Elissa promised cheerfully. "What about it? We can leave right after work and meet him in the lounge of that hotel up the street. He'll be delighted to make your acquaintance."

"Well . . ."

"Come on, Marie, I'll be there, too!" Elissa smiled winningly.

"If you think he won't feel like I'm being pushed at him . . ."

"Trust me."

Marie suddenly grinned. "Okay, Elissa. If I can't trust you in a situation like this, who can I trust?"

It would be easy, Elissa decided a few minutes later as she hung up the phone after speaking to Dean. She and Marie would make a quiet exit from the office promptly at five. Wade, who always worked an hour or so later than the rest of his staff, wouldn't even know. If he chose to stop by her apartment during the evening, she would be home. The business with Dean and Marie would only take a few minutes. Elissa was very efficient at handling easy situations like this.

The buzzing of her office intercom interrupted the smooth flow of her plans.

"Elissa?"

She swallowed, taken aback. "Yes, Wade?"

"I'm going to be able to get away for lunch, after all. I'll meet you at the elevators at twelve. You will hold the door for me this time, won't you, honey?" he added as if it were an afterthought.

She sighed. "Yes, Wade."

"I thought you would. We'll go down to Pioneer Square."

Many more calls like that one, Elissa thought disgustedly, and Wade wouldn't have to wait until Sunday to make the engagement announcement! The office rumor mill would do the job for him.

There were a few covert glances of surprise and interest at noon when Wade coolly guided Elissa into the elevator, but no one had the nerve to ask any questions. Elissa was grateful when the majority of the crowd spilled out at the lobby floor, on their way to nearby restaurants for lunch. She and Wade continued silently down to the parking garage where the sleek Jaguar waited for its master.

"You've certainly learned your way around Seattle in a hurry," she remarked politely as he nosed the car out onto the street and headed for the restored older part of the city. The historic section, once a bustling meeting place for men on their way to the Klondike gold rush or those involved in the lumber business, was now a popular complex of galleries, shops, and restaurants. The fine old architecture had been preserved, along with cobblestone parks now filled with a host of colorful street people who regarded the well-dressed business crowd tolerantly.

"Somebody in the office mentioned an interesting little restaurant down here." Wade smiled. "I believe he said it qualified as romantic."

Elissa flushed, glancing out the window at the brick and stone buildings dating from the nineteenth century. "Is that why you chose it?"

"Don't you think I'm romantic?" he demanded, offended.

She pretended to consider that, pursing her lips provocatively. "No," she finally announced. "I'd say you were pragmatic, not romantic!"

"Just goes to show how much you still have to learn about me!"

The restaurant was a delightful little spot tucked away in the corner of an elegant red-brick building, its decor done with an early Seattle theme.

"I'm surprised you're able to find time to get away today," Elissa murmured noncommittally as she perused the menu. "I thought you'd be busy with that crowd from Oregon."

"The lumber firm? They called and asked

if they could meet to discuss computerizing their records after lunch instead of during lunch," Wade said. "It will probably tie me up a bit this afternoon, so I may be late getting away from work. Thought I'd better take advantage of the free lunch hour to see you."

"I'm flattered," she said dryly, her eyes laughing at him as he glanced up speculatively.

"No, you're not," he contradicted. "You're used to people rearranging their schedules for you."

"Not true! You have a very low opinion of me, don't you, Wade Taggert?" she grumbled.

"A realistic one. I think I'm going to have the veal. How about you?"

She sighed thoughtfully. "I'm not very hungry."

"Nervous about Sunday night?" he queried solicitously.

"Should I be?" she managed gamely.

"No," he said with sudden, unexpected gentleness, his gray eyes warming. "I'll take care of everything. There's nothing at all to worry about."

Elissa stared at him for a timeless, whirling moment and then took a grip on her senses. She would not allow this man to drag her under, damn it!

"I'm sure everything will go very smoothly," she agreed quietly and tried to still her pulses as they began to race under the heat of his gaze.

His words were still on her mind that afternoon as Elissa collected her belongings and her friend Marie.

"I'm still not sure about this, Elissa," Marie whispered nervously as they entered the dark lounge together. The expensive well-upholstered room was beginning to come alive with the normal Friday after-work crowd, and Elissa automatically searched the ranks of business suits, seeking Dean Norwood's cheerful face.

"Don't worry, Marie, I'll take care of everything," Elissa assured her friend, realizing with a flicker of humor that she was using the same words Wade had used to her earlier in the day.

"Elissa! Over here!" Dean's call came cheerfully through the murmur of voices, and she turned to see him guarding a small table. She lifted a hand in acknowledgment and started forward, Marie following hesitantly at her heels.

"Glad you could make it, Dean. I want you to meet a friend of mine. Would you believe it? She's into sailing!"

With easy grace and natural skill, Elissa

made the introductions and then carefully began to guide the conversation. In a very few moments she was no longer even a part of the discussion as it flowed happily between the other two. Things were going very nicely, she decided with satisfaction. Of course, her task had been simplified by the knowledge that both her friends were interested in sailing, she admitted modestly. Still . . . The corner of her mouth lifted with self-mockery as she wondered whether or not there really was any magic involved. It was all so easy!

She stayed long enough to make sure Dean and Marie were safely headed in the right direction and then smoothly injected her apologies into the conversation.

"I've got to be on my way." She smiled fondly, getting easily to her feet and reaching out for her coat. "You two have a good time, and I'll see you both soon."

"Oh, Elissa, must you go?" Marie looked momentarily startled to find herself in such a comfortable, casual situation with an attractive male.

"I'm afraid so," Elissa said with light regret. "I've got a thousand and one things to do this evening, and I . . ."

"And she didn't want to have her fiancé catch her having a drink with another man," interposed a familiar gravelly voice that sent instant chills down Elissa's spine. She whirled to find Wade less than a foot away, directly behind her. He seemed very large and very dangerous in the dark room.

"Wade!" she gasped, striving to regain control of the situation. "I didn't see you . . ."

"I gathered that much," he noted wryly, taking the belt of her coat out of her nervous fingers and cinching it tightly at her waist. The intimate task brought him very close indeed, and she was violently aware of the leashed anger in him.

"Fiancé?" Dean's mildly confused question interrupted the tension for an instant.

"We're making it official Sunday evening," Wade declared quietly, his eyes flicking from Dean's surprised expression to Marie's curious one. "I trust you'll be coming, Marie? That's what the invitation to my house is all about. You did get it along with the rest of the staff this afternoon?" he added politely, ignoring Elissa.

"Yes, sir," Marie responded immediately, her gaze going at once to her supervisor's flushed face. "I'll definitely be there. We all wondered what it was about. . . ."

"Actually," Wade purred deeply, his arm tightening around Elissa's waist, "it's supposed to be something of a surprise announcement. I'd appreciate it if you didn't give the game away until I put the ring on her finger Sunday night."

"Oh, no, sir." Marie smiled nervously. "I won't say a word!" And she wouldn't either, Elissa realized grimly. The staff was far too much in awe of their new boss to risk his displeasure.

"Elissa, I had no idea . . ." Dean said, frowning slightly as he looked up and met her eyes.

"It's been very . . . very sudden, Dean," she said hurriedly, aware of Wade's slanting, mocking glance. "I hope you'll congratulate me."

"Yes, I suppose so," he began uncertainly, his eyes shifting from her features to Wade's implacable face. "But why didn't you mention it earlier? I thought, I mean . . ."

Damn Wade! Elissa thought savagely. He had ruined everything!

"I'm afraid I'm guilty of rushing her off her feet," the subject of her heated thoughts murmured with patently false apology. "Aren't I, honey?"

"Yes," she bit out and then saw the confusion on Dean's face increase. First things first, she told herself resolutely, turning away from Wade's enigmatic gaze. "Dean,

I'm sorry about this. I hope you'll understand . . ."

With every bit of skill she possessed, Elissa sought to project a wistful, hopeful plea for understanding and friendship as she smiled tremulously at her former boyfriend. "I wanted you to be the first to know, but you and Marie seemed to be so involved with your conversation I didn't quite get a chance to bring up my little surprise."

"Was that why you called me and asked me to meet you here after work?" Dean asked, frowning slightly as he considered developments.

"As I said, I was going to explain everything, but I didn't feel right interrupting . . ." She looked sadly at him and felt Wade's hand clenched into her waist. He knew exactly what she was doing, and he was letting her know he was aware of it. Deliberately she forced a brighter smile.

"I brought Marie along because she's a friend of mine who needs to get out more," Elissa went on chattily. "She's had some bad times lately, and I thought your company might cheer her up, Dean. You're so much fun."

"I see," he said slowly, clearly confused, perhaps a bit upset, but more than willing to try the obvious escape route Elissa was extending. "I'm sorry you didn't get a chance to tell me your news," he went on, nodding as if it really had been his fault. "I certainly wish you the best. And don't worry about Marie, here; we seem to have a lot in common. . . ." He turned a broad smile on his companion, who smiled back at first self-consciously and then with genuine enthusiasm.

A perfect match, Elissa thought. If only Wade hadn't spoiled it! But it looked as if matters were going to sort themselves out after all.

"You two won't mind if I remove my fiancée from the discussion, will you?" Wade was saying equably. "She and I have a lot to discuss. You know how it is. So many last-minute details . . ." He let the sentence trail off suggestively, easing Elissa away as the other two nodded politely.

Before she could say another word, Wade had somehow put a great deal of distance between Elissa and her two companions. And with every step, the sinewy muscles of his arm seemed to tighten more and more forcefully. By the time they reached the foggy street, Elissa could barely breathe.

"Of all the stupid, poorly timed, oafish things to do!" she hissed, struggling for breath. "What in the world did you think you were doing? I had everything so neatly set up! It was all going so perfectly . . . !"

"If I were you," he informed her bluntly, half guiding, half dragging her to where the Jaguar crouched at the curb, "I'd be very careful about throwing a tantrum just now. It wouldn't take much to convince me I ought to chew the hell out of you right here in front of the whole world!"

"You'd have absolutely no right!" Elissa began imperiously and then found herself stuffed ungently into the front seat and the door slammed on her angry words. She didn't let that stop her. As soon as he opened his own door and slid behind the wheel, she picked up where she had left off.

"I wasn't doing anything wrong, even by your exalted standards, Mr. Taggert," she gritted loftily.

"You call meeting another man for a drink doing nothing wrong?" he charged coolly, pulling out into traffic with a smooth caution that belied his obviously irate state of mind.

"I wasn't meeting another man for a drink, damn it! I was . . . I was trying to arrange something." She stumbled over the explanation, because what she had tried to arrange *had* involved meeting another man for a drink.

What was wrong with her? Why should she feel even faintly guilty? She owed no loyalty to this man — only the promise of revenge! Confused and appalled by the unnerving realization that Wade was making her feel guilty, Elissa sought refuge in a more heated tirade.

"I was trying to casually introduce Marie and Dean," she went on bitterly. "I thought the two of them would be perfect together. What's wrong with a little matchmaking?"

He threw her a derisive glance. "Nothing, as long as I'm going to supervise."

"Well, I could hardly have brought you along," she muttered. "Having the boss around doesn't make for the most relaxed of atmospheres. As it is, you came very close to ruining everything. I can only hope that, between the two of them, they'll be able to salvage the situation. I thought you were going to work late this evening, anyway," she added belatedly.

"Is that the reason you picked this evening to meet Norwood?" he retorted coolly, his eyes on the traffic. "Because you thought I was safely out of the way?"

"I was not meeting Dean!"

"Strange," he murmured laconically, "that's certainly what it looked like when I walked into that lounge. For one very dramatic moment, I thought you might be up to your old trick of meeting men on the sly in local bars." Some hint of warning in his voice shook her.

"What a horrible thing to say!" she gasped, outraged.

"It was a horrible thing to contemplate, I assure you," he returned a little too casually.

Elissa shot him a questioning glance. Something didn't quite fit here. Wade was clearly disapproving of the situation, but he wasn't in the rage she might have expected if he really had thought she was meeting Dean behind his back.

"And what about you?" she gibed deliberately. "Were you up to your old trick of tailing your employees to local lounges?"

"I came looking for you just after you'd left the building. One of the women in your group was still there, and she remembered Marie talking about having a drink with you after work. She also remembered the name of the place, and of course as soon as she mentioned it . . ."

"You remembered that was where I was in the habit of carrying on my illicit affair with Martin Randolph!"

"You can't blame me for being a little upset by the prospect of you heading off to the nearest swinging lounge after work," he pointed out calmly.

"And when you saw Dean at our table, you put two and two together and came up with three!" she exploded.

"Very nearly," he admitted with a quirking downturn of his mouth.

"What do you mean, 'very nearly'?" she demanded suspiciously.

"Elissa," he said with such quiet intent that her blood ran cold, "when I first saw you and Dean at the same table I was ready to tear him limb from limb and then drag you home and go to work on you!"

She blinked. "What happened? Did you decide to forgo your macho vengeance on him and be satisfied with taking it out on me, instead?" she parried nervously.

"No, fortunately I realized what was going on as I neared the table. It was the way you had neatly engineered the two of them together and the way you were preparing to leave, looking like the satisfied cat that had swallowed the cream. You looked so enormously pleased with yourself I realized you must have intended for Marie and Dean to hit it off."

Elissa blinked again, this time in astonishment. "You mean . . . you mean you aren't really upset? You believe me?"

"I believe you," he assured her dryly. "That doesn't mean I'm not feeling mildly provoked by the whole thing."

"But if you understood what I was doing . . ." she began uncertainly.

"There's something about watching you work your charms that makes a man like me uneasy," he confessed ruefully. "Especially when there's another man involved. I prefer to be around when you're spellcasting. It's safer that way. Which brings me to the one point I want to make this evening," he ended on a drawl.

"Which is?" Elissa began to relax. She was feeling much more comfortable now that she knew Wade believed her. She wouldn't have to fret over his reactions much longer, she told herself encouraging, but until the final showdown Sunday evening perhaps she would watch her step.

"Which is that you're not going to go off on your own after work to the nearest singles bar," he concluded in a steady, ironclad tone that brooked no argument.

Foolishly, Elissa tried to argue anyway. "I wasn't alone. I had Marie with me!"

"That doesn't make one damn bit of difference, and you know it," he told her grimly. "If you're going to go out in the evenings from now on, it will be with me. Two women roaming a singles scene doesn't strike me as any more appropriate than one. Especially when one of those two women is engaged to be married. If I ever catch you wandering off like that again, Elissa, there will be hell to pay. Is that very clear?"

She heard the icy command in his voice and considered it carefully. It occurred to her that she was getting off rather lightly, especially when one took into account the mood Wade must have been in when he first entered the lounge and saw her with Dean. And there were only two more days until the grand moment of revenge. Yes, she could afford to subside meekly.

"Yes, Wade," she husked, glancing down at her hands in her lap. She was surprised to find the palms slightly damp.

"That's it." Abruptly he smiled. "You're learning."

"Learning what?" she snapped, goaded by his easy acceptance of victory.

"Learning that there are limits to my good-natured patience," he explained innocently.

"Good-natured patience!" she rasped. "That's the last way I would describe your temperament!" Her hair swirled lightly about her ears as she whipped her head around to glare across the seat at him.

"I'll admit I don't go to the lengths you do to ensure everyone's pleasant state of mind," he acknowledged honestly. "I would never, for example, go out of my way to ensure that a former girlfriend found herself a new romance before telling her we were finished. I wonder if Dean will ever realize just how much you did for him? Probably not. Why did you do it, Elissa? Is it just instinctive now to make sure everyone is contented? Has it become an automatic part of your charm? Everyone except me, of course," he added as an obvious afterthought. "I seem to be excluded from the list of people whose happiness you so charmingly concern yourself with."

"You don't seem unduly worried about being left out," she declared tartly.

"I'm not. Yet."

"Meaning you might be someday?" she persisted sweetly.

"Someday, yes," he agreed as he pulled up in front of her apartment building and switched off the engine. He turned in the seat to face her squarely, the gray gaze full of assessing study as he raked her rebellious expression. "But not just yet. Right now I regard your failure to soothe my poor ego as a hopeful sign."

"Grasping at straws?" she asked kindly.

"No, simply analyzing the situation." He half smiled, stroking her cheek with one lazy finger. "Right now it's fine with me to learn I'm an unsettling influence in your life. You need that sort of unsettling. At any rate, it's bound to hold your attention until I can . . ." He broke off, and Elissa was startled to see a dark flush creep up his tanned neck. In the limited light of the streetlamp she thought at first she might have been mistaken, but her instincts told her she wasn't.

"Until you can what, Wade?" she inquired with chilling politeness.

"Until I can terminate the hunt," he growled determinedly. "Come here and kiss me!"

She tipped her head to one side. "Why should I kiss you after the way you embarrassed me in that lounge?"

"You should kiss me out of gratitude that I didn't cause a much bigger scene," he observed dryly, gray eyes mocking.

"A kiss of gratitude," she said reflectively, studying the hard line of his mouth. "I'm not sure I feel that grateful."

"Would you like me to impress upon you how close you were walking to the edge tonight?" he invited softly.

"When are you going to stop threatening

me every time you don't get your own way, Mr. Taggert?" Elissa whispered, supremely aware of the tension and intimacy of the moment.

"When I'm sure you're well and truly trussed in my net," he retorted throatily. "Come, Elissa. Kiss your fiancé, who went so easy on you tonight when he had every right to read you the riot act."

"And if I don't?" she hazarded provocatively, aware of the thrilling challenge in him — a challenge that reached to the core of her femininity. "What happens if I don't throw myself into your arms out of sheer relief and gratitude?"

"Guess," he invited succinctly, not moving.

Unconsciously, Elissa nibbled on her lower lip. "Threats, threats, and more threats," she groaned on a mere breath of sound.

"Which you might be able to offset with kisses, kisses, and more kisses," he retorted, watching her face in the dim light. He seemed fascinated by the green glow of her eyes.

"A calculated risk," she noted, equally fascinated by the play of shadows on the uncompromising lines of his face.

"Very calculated," he agreed.

Very delicately, not quite certain what was

driving her to do it, Elissa touched the tip of her finger to the corner of his mouth, and then she leaned forward to drop the lightest of butterfly kisses on his lips.

The small kiss had a strangely hypnotic affect on her senses. When he didn't move or make any attempt to reach for her, she tried another one. Her fingertips slid along the line of his jaw to rest behind his head, entrenching themselves in the darkness of his hair. Deliberately she pulled his head a fraction closer, her mouth beginning to move more boldly on his. She bared her teeth and gently closed them around his lower lip in the silkiest of daring caresses.

Instantly the world exploded around her as she was pushed heavily back into the rich leather seat. The weight of his chest settled over hers and he seemed to glory in the feel of her softly crushed breasts. The strong, probing fingers of his hand bit into her thigh just as his mouth forced her lips apart.

Wade had one hand behind her neck, holding her head still in the crook of his arm, and the hand on her thigh began moving upward, undoing the buttons of her blouse as it went.

"Please, Wade!" But whether she was going to plead for him not to make love to her on a city street or whether she was going to beg him to continue, Elissa could never be certain. The rest of her words were lost in the warmth of his invading tongue.

And then his hands were invading the small valley between her breasts, claiming the territory there with a possessiveness that left her weak and clinging.

"Elissa, I want you so much." He breathed hotly against her skin as he buried his face in her throat. "Do you have any idea what you do to me? You make me want to take you, to make love to you so completely you'll never, ever forget who owns you!"

She tried to protest and couldn't find the strength. When his lips moved lower until he curled a tongue almost painfully around one vulnerable nipple, she drew in her breath with a desperate impatience. It was hard, so very hard, to think of revenge or anything else when he took her in his arms like this. All she wanted was to give and go on giving until she had taken her fill of him.

"Your body comes to my call so quickly now," he rasped thickly, sliding his hand along the curve of her thigh and up under her wool skirt until she was shivering with the implied promise. "Soon every part of you will answer to me, and you'll see you have to take me into your castle!"

"Wade, oh, Wade." His name was torn from her in short, panting gasps of pleasure and excitement. But even as she was pressing herself more tightly against his hardness, she sensed him begin to pull away.

"Calm yourself, little one," he soothed, beginning to stroke his fingers through her hair in a quieting action that left her at once confused and a little angry. "We can't continue this here. We'll go upstairs to your apartment where I can undress you properly and see you lying naked on the bed, waiting for me!" The gray eyes burned with silver flames as he raked her love-softened face. Without another word, he reached for the door handle, his intent violently clear.

"No, Wade," she managed chokingly, desperately striving to bring her senses back under control. "No . . . you can't come up with me. Not tonight!" She hated the hint of panic in her voice, but it seemed to serve the purpose of stopping him cold.

"Why not, Elissa?" he growled tightly. "You want me as much as I want you. There's no way you can hide your reaction!"

"I don't have to explain myself to you!"

she stormed, scrambling to rebutton her blouse. "It's a woman's right to call a halt to the lovemaking, and I'm exercising my right!"

Nervously she met his ravaging gaze, uncertain what he would do and knowing she wouldn't be able to stop him if he chose to drag her up to the apartment over her protests. And how long would she protest? she wondered forlornly.

With a small gesture of ruthless power held deliberately in check, Wade tapped the car keys against the leather-covered dash. She could almost see him making up his mind, and the silent tension in the car was frightening.

"All right, Elissa," he finally said in a voice that echoed the small gesture with the keys. "If you're sure this is the way you want it . . ."

"It is, Wade. Please?" She forced herself to tack on the last word with a suitably beseeching gaze. God! What was happening to her? How could she be behaving like this? The whole dangerous business was threatening to overwhelm her, she realized. Thank heaven it would all come to an end on Sunday. She couldn't take much more of this highly refined torture!

Wade took one last look into her storm-tossed eyes and got out of the car. Without a word more on the subject, he took her politely up to her apartment and left her at the door.

Chapter 10

Saturday evening once more found Elissa waiting with a mix of emotions for the arrival of Wade Taggert. Restlessly she paced the floor, the clinging skirts of her sleekly cut green dress outlining her legs lovingly as she moved. Time was running out, overtaking her in a mad rush that threatened her sense of control. A sense she had always taken for granted before encountering Wade, she reminded herself duly.

Tomorrow night she had to have her revenge neatly packaged and ready to be delivered. She paused in front of the mirror and grimaced wryly at her reflection. It was all happening too fast! She wasn't quite ready . . .

"But how much more ready do you want to be, friend?" she demanded of her counterpart in the mirror. "There is a safety factor involved here!"

And that safety factor was tied up with how much longer she could expect Wade to refrain from pushing the physical side of their relationship. Even now she didn't fully understand how she'd managed to hold him at bay. She had been successful only because he hadn't forced the issue, she admitted with a massive amount of self-honesty. There was no understanding it, but since the night she'd tricked him into offering marriage, he had seemed willing to give in to her on this one point.

Of course, the momentous occasion of her marriage proposal had only occurred a few nights ago, she thought morosely, turning away from the mirror with a frown. There was always tonight. . . .

"What the hell's the matter with you, Elissa Sheldon?" she muttered, resuming her pacing. "You should be glad you haven't had to fight that particular battle down to the last ditch. There's a damn good chance you would have lost, and you know it!" Memories of how close she had come to letting him make love to her the previous evening washed over her.

The thoughts brought a flush to her face and a tremor to her full mouth. She clamped her teeth on her lower lip to still the latter. It wasn't fair that the one man in the world who had ever brought her to this stage of excitement and despair and wonder was a man who thought the worst of her. A man who was only marrying her because he assumed that was the price he had to pay to have her. Elissa's fingers closed into fists at her sides. The world had always been fair to her. Why this?

She must think of her revenge, she decided, stopping her pacing as the bell rang. She must keep her mind on dealing with the scene she would be creating tomorrow evening. The excitement was in her eyes when she opened the door to Wade.

"I've noticed you've hidden my painting," he complained an hour later as he seated her gallantly in the exquisite Continental restaurant with its intimate, seductive atmosphere. "Is it finished?" he demanded with a distinct hunger in his eyes as he sat down across from her.

"It's finished," she allowed, for some reason unable to resist a smile at his expectancy. She reached for her linen napkin and spread it gracefully in her lap as the waiter arrived with the white wine Wade had ordered be brought while he considered the menus. She decided against telling her escort that she had finished the painting in a strange rage of emotion after he had left her on Friday night.

"Where are you keeping it? In your bedroom? I'd like to think it was in there." He grinned unrepentantly, raising his glass to clink it gently against hers. "After all, I'm keeping the one I had Hal do for you in my bedroom."

"What?" She stared at him, floored by this news. "You've commissioned a picture for me? For our wedding?" For some reason the information took her completely aback.

"Poor Elissa." He chuckled, sipping his wine and watching her over the rim of the glass. "You're so used to relationships in which you give precisely what you want to give and take so carefully what you want in return that the person you're taking from doesn't even know what he's given. Doesn't it intrigue you a bit to know you're going to be getting something from me that you hadn't even guessed existed? Something you hadn't even thought you desired? I phoned Hal the night after your party, you know, and told him what I wanted. I brought it back with me from California."

"More witch baiting?" she murmured, the corner of her mouth quirking as she considered his unexpected comment.

"I prefer to think of it as witch tempting," he corrected. "Remember the special toys I told you about that day you came for the picnic? Toys to tempt a witch."

"You also said they might be dangerous, I

believe," Elissa breathed, knowing the intoxication of bantering with this man and wondering what it would be like when he was gone from her life. When she had *evicted* him from it, she hurriedly rephrased her thoughts.

"I'll be around to make sure you don't get into any trouble you can't handle with them." Wade smiled with undisguised masculine anticipation.

"I've never had much trouble handling toys or anything else before you came along," Elissa couldn't resist putting in spiritedly. If this was to be her last real night with Wade Taggert, why shouldn't she enjoy herself? It had been an interesting interlude in an otherwise comfortable, serene life, she decided.

"But have you had much fun or excitement with your toys?" he pressed, the wolf smile in his eyes now.

"Life's always gone rather smoothly," she countered, taking a sip of her wine. "I don't recall ever wanting for anything."

"It's when you want something that it gets exciting," Wade told her with cool authority.

"Desire is a fleeting thing," she pointed out quietly. "Especially for a man."

"It depends on exactly what is desired.

Some things can be taken, used, and forgotten. Other things . . ." His sentence hovered, unfinished, in the air between them.

"Do you know in advance which things go into the long-lasting category?" She quipped.

"I'm a man, not a boy," he told her softly. "I know which things go where in my life."

She studied him for a moment, feeling the tension and unspoken bonds being woven between them. "What long-lasting desires have you known?" she asked at last, unable to stop the words.

"My work is the main one, I suppose. The one I've taken the most effort to satisfy," he replied unhesitatingly.

"No women?" she dared carefully.

"There have been women," he answered easily, unselfconsciously, and uncaringly. "But none in the long-lasting category. Are you asking which category you'll be in?" He watched the color stain her throat and cheeks.

"You've already told me the answer to that," she said with all the neutrality she could muster.

"I don't believe we've ever set a specific ending date to our relationship," he contradicted. She could hear the deliberate temptation in his words and grimly ignored it.

"Would you like to talk about it?" he invited, his gray eyes gleaming with intent.

"No." Elissa didn't hesitate. The last thing she wanted to discuss this evening was the end of their relationship. If he only knew just how soon it was going to come to an end, she reminded herself, trying to feel triumph. The feeling wouldn't come. "I think I'd rather hear about the long-lasting things in your life," she continued. "Tell me about your work, first. Have you always known what you wanted to do?"

"I've always known I wanted to wield power of the sort I've got at CompuDesign," he said without any apology. "Does that make me some kind of animal or renegade?"

"It makes you a wolf, and you know it." She smiled.

He shrugged. "So be it. I need the conflict and the day-to-day assertion of my own abilities."

"Does politics interest you?" Elissa asked curiously.

"Lord, no!" he exclaimed, his mouth twisting wryly. "I couldn't stand the constant compromise and the need to answer to a constituency. Give me the jungle of the boardroom and the marketplace any day!"

"Yes," she agreed abruptly, nodding. "You're far too much the lone wolf to ever fit into the political arena. In this day and age I suppose the business world is the best place for you. You're fortunate in knowing yourself so well." And then she thought of his stark, bleak paintings. "But it isn't all excitement and adventure for you, is it?"

"What brought that up?"

"I was thinking of those paintings you have hanging in your home," she told him, striving for some degree of lightness in her words.

"Ah, yes. The loneliness you think you see in my art selection," he murmured, turning his wineglass to catch the light from the candle on the table. He watched the wine and not her as he spoke.

"Has your taste in art always leaned in the direction of the style you have in your town house?" she persisted, unable to let the subject rest even though he was not encouraging her to talk about it.

"I only became interested in art a few years ago," he said, lifting his eyes back to hers. "But, yes, I think the two in my living room are typical of my taste. My eye for technical skill has improved, but the images are similar to those which attracted me from the first."

Was that the real reason he had decided to take the plunge into marriage? Elissa asked herself with a jolt of stunned dismay. To counteract the loneliness? The thought was an unwelcome one. She wanted to think of Wade Taggert as trying to use her to satisfy one of his temporary desires. It would be so much easier to punish him for what he had done to her if that was the case.

"What about you, Elissa?" he interrupted her agitated thoughts to inquire with what sounded like genuine curiosity. The gray gaze pinned her. "Have your paintings always been of other worlds and the kind of adventure you can't know in this one?"

She produced a little half smile as she thought about the question. No one had ever asked it before. "I don't know what attracts me to that kind of adventure. Heaven knows I should have outgrown it years ago. I thought for a while of trying to write tales like the kind I read, but somehow I discovered painting instead. It lets me create the kinds of scenes that appeal to me. While I'm painting I sort of weave a story in my mind, a story for which the picture represents the main scene in the tale . . ." Elissa broke off, flushing slightly. "It's hard to explain," she mumbled apologetically.

"Only because you've never tried to do it before, I'll bet." Wade grinned, reaching across the table to fit his large hand over her smaller one. "What about your work?" A shuttered look descended on the silvery pools of his eyes. "How did you get into technical writing?"

She laughed at that. "I fell into it. The same way I fell into an English major in college. I fall into a lot of things in life."

"And always land on your feet?"

"Always!" she shot back with a touch of warning.

"And now you're falling into marriage. With a wolf, at that," he noted slowly.

"It is a little outside my normal activities."

"Not comfortable?" he teased.

"It hasn't been so far! Tell me something, Wade," she drawled deliberately. "What would your reaction have been if our positions had been reversed? If I, as your boss, had told you I wasn't going to give you a promotion you deserved because I wanted to teach you a lesson?"

His face hardened perceptibly, and she knew she'd succeeded in taking him by surprise.

"To tell you the truth, I hadn't considered it from that point of view," he owned gently, the gray eyes alert and wary.

"It gives a person pause, doesn't it?" she observed dryly as the waiter appeared to take their order.

The small consultation which took place

over the issue of which fish was fresh and what salad dressing was desired broke the tension of the moment, but it floated back into place the instant the waiter disappeared again.

"I like to think," Wade stated tersely, "that I would have had the good grace to accept the lesson."

"Always assuming you were guilty of having tried to obtain the position by illicit means in the first place!" Elissa smiled brilliantly, sensing a hint of victory.

"Of course," he agreed aloofly.

She leaned forward, the brilliant smile still in place, her blue-green eyes gleaming with derision and laughter. "You know what I think?"

"What?" he asked, clearly sensing danger.

"I think you would have raised hell. Perhaps committed murder. Or at the very least torn CompuDesign apart before storming out the door!" Elissa sat back, grinning triumphantly.

"Regardless of whether I was innocent or guilty?" he hedged.

"Yes!"

"You may be right." He capitulated without even a struggle, and that proved quite disappointing to Elissa, who had been looking for a battle she knew she could win. It was his turn to grin, a slashing smile which held no hint of defeat. "It's fortunate for me you're of a different temperament, isn't it?"

Elissa steered clear of such dangerous subjects for the rest of the meal, chatting willingly about art and Wade's acclimatization to the dampness of a Seattle winter.

"Do you miss California?" she asked at one point during dessert, a luscious cream with a caramelized topping.

"No," he confessed without hesitation. And that was that. They went on to discuss other matters, and then Wade rose to lead her into the lounge.

"Do you realize we're on the verge of being married and we've never even danced together?" he demanded feelingly as he took her into his arms on the dance floor.

"Perhaps we're, uh, rushing matters," Elissa took the opportunity to suggest even as she floated against him.

"There's no such thing as rushing matters," he informed her gravely, tightening his hold until she was deeply aware of him with all her senses. The spicy hint of aftershave mingled with the clean, earthy smell of his body. The rough texture of his suit jacket was somehow enticing against her cheek. But most seductive of all was the elemental feminine pleasure to be derived from being held by a man strong enough and ruthless enough to protect the woman of his choice. Elissa tried to force the fantasy from her mind but had little luck.

"What do you mean by that?" she asked, sensing his enjoyment in touching her hair with his lips.

"I mean that either a thing is right or it isn't. If it's right, then why not rush it?"

"Do you always see life in such simple terms?" She laughed, lifting her face to meet his eyes.

"It . . ." He paused, and she heard the laughter deep in his chest. "It *simplifies* things!"

"Spoken like a true lone wolf." She sighed against his shoulder. "Two ways of approaching everything: your way and the wrong way!"

"Perhaps I'll be able to pick up some tips on handling life with more finesse from you," he offered encouragingly in her ear. "Have I told you where we're going on our honeymoon?" he went on deliberately.

Elissa, who had not thought about anything past Sunday night all day, missed a step and wound up planting the toe of her shoe on top of his instep.

"I take it that's a negative response?" he remarked imperturbably.

"You know very well you haven't mentioned the issue!"

"I thought we'd take the first few days of next week off and seclude ourselves in Victoria."

"Go to Canada? In the winter?" She raised her head again at that.

"I doubt that the weather up in British Columbia is much worse than it is down here, and this is off season for Victoria. I can have you all to myself in front of a cozy fire in a proper old British inn. . . ."

"For someone who comes from California, you appear to know a great deal about Victoria!" she chided, trying to assimilate the thought of a honeymoon.

"Umm," he agreed. "I made the reservations yesterday. A place Conway in marketing mentioned. Victoria's supposed to be the most British part of Canada. We'll stuff ourselves on tea and scones and crumpets. The inn I've booked is noted for the genuine antiques in the bedrooms and high tea every afternoon. Sound good?"

"Would it matter if I didn't approve?" she shot back tartly, slanting a glance up at him from beneath her lashes.

He looked hurt. "I thought you'd like the place."

"Does it ever occur to you to ask someone

else's opinion once in a while?" she teased, unable to continue protesting once she'd seen the hurt in his eyes. "Lucky I like Victoria in the winter!"

"I thought you would." He smiled and pulled her head down against his shoulder, and Elissa quietly began to panic.

On the drive home much later Elissa settled sleepily back into the leather seat of the Jag and watched the lights of the city through half-shut eyes. She was absorbed in her problems, which seemed to have become greatly magnified during the course of the evening, and didn't notice for a while that the route Wade was pursuing would not lead back to her apartment. She considered the various ramifications of that piece of information and wondered how to bring up the subject subtly.

"Where are we going?" It was difficult to be subtle about such a question.

"Home," he told her easily, sending a quick, amused smile across the seat before returning his attention to his driving.

"Your home. Not mine." She waited, her nerves beginning to tingle with a strange, unwelcome expectancy. The same expectancy that was starting to become very familiar around Wade Taggert. A dangerous, beckoning thing. She remembered unwillingly what he'd said about dangerous and tempting toys for a witch.

"My home," he confirmed unhesitatingly. And then he asked softly, captivatingly, "Afraid?"

"Should I be?"

"No." His voice was still soft. "As of Monday it will be your home, too."

Some of the panic Elissa had experienced earlier returned. She could feel it crawling along her nerves. But it was having to fight another emotion for space. A weakening, acquiescent urge to forget about Sunday night; to simply go home with Wade tonight and see where it all would lead . . . But she knew the answer to that, Elissa tried to tell herself. Agreeing to go home with Wade even for a nightcap was a tacit agreement to staying the night with him. Who was she kidding when she tried to imagine herself only staying for a drink and then leaving? She bit her lip in the darkness of the car and wondered what was the matter with her. Why wasn't she telling Wade she wanted to go back to her own apartment? She could handle the situation adroitly enough there, she thought. Give him a good-night drink and send him on his way, exactly as she had handled Dean Norwood earlier in the week. But Wade wasn't Dean, and Elissa wasn't at all sure she could edge him coolly out the door when the time came. That admission more than anything else seemed to sap her will to argue with him about being driven to his town house.

There was a curious, intimate silence in the car as the Jag sped through the city night. Elissa couldn't bring herself to break it, and Wade showed no interest in doing so, either. Every block which passed was taking her that much deeper into enemy territory. Enemy? Elissa considered that. Surely she had the ability to deal with an enemy on his own terrain. She was no coward, and she had a goal: Sunday night. She lifted her chin and unclenched the fingers in her lap. She could afford to go home with Wade this evening because she could handle the situation. She could handle anyone!

A few minutes later, Wade parked the elegant car in the drive, opened his door and paused to turn and smile at Elissa, who sat very still as the light came on in the Jag. He said nothing, but the heart-stopping smile and the warmth in his eyes told the whole story. An ancient story of magic and sorcery on the most fundamental level. Elissa swallowed and felt the muscles and bones of her body begin to melt. A second later he was out of the car and striding around to open her door.

"Honey, you're trembling!" he said with immediate concern as he tucked her against him, his arm wrapped around her like a band of steel. But the steel felt protective, not imprisoning, she realized dazedly as he walked her toward the front door. Desperately she tried to rally her scattered forces by reminding them that was the most dangerous mistake of all. She must not delude herself into believing Wade's feeling toward her had changed. She was still only a woman he had decided he wanted. Wanted badly enough to agree to the price he thought she was asking.

"It's cold," she mumbled by way of explaining the trembling.

He pulled her close against the heat of his body, and she could feel his smile above her head. "We'll get you inside and I'll fix you a nice hot toddy. You'll be warm enough soon. I promise!"

The depth of meaning in his last words nearly caused Elissa to stumble. But even if she had, he probably wouldn't have noticed; he was holding her too tightly. She stood pressing her cheek into the roughness of his coat while he fished out his keys and opened the door. He felt so good, she thought wonderingly. What would it have been like if he'd fallen in love with her? If he hadn't believed her capable of the sneaky, conniving behavior of which he'd accused her? It was such a temptation to forget the origins of their relationship and give herself up to the moment. The door opened, and she was pushed gently inside.

For an instant Elissa stood staring at the harsh seascape which had first caught her attention on the day she had come to his house for the picnic. Did lone wolves ever seek mates? The door closed behind her, and she turned to watch as he dropped his keys onto a nearby table and pulled off his suit coat.

"Poor little Elissa," he murmured on a note of affectionate humor as he tossed the coat aside and came forward to cup her face in his hands. "You look confused and cold and about to melt at my feet." The silvery gaze swept her face.

"I could hardly be cold and about to melt at the same time," she said with an attempt at some sophistication and lightness.

"No? It's possible to feel two conflicting emotions at the same time. Why not two conflicting sensations?" Wade's mouth curved into what was probably meant to be a smile of reassurance but which managed to increase Elissa's uncertainty. It showed in the jewel brightness of the gaze she turned up to meet his.

"I'll get you that hot drink," he whispered, bending his head to drop a small kiss on her nose. "Then I'll build a fire and we can talk." His hands dropped from her face, and he turned to walk toward the kitchen. Elissa followed slowly.

"Talk about what?" They had been talking all evening. What was left to discuss at this hour?

"About us. Why don't you find something you like in my record collection and put it on the stereo while I get the toddies?"

Grateful for the small task which would keep her from standing in the kitchen doorway and staring at him, Elissa wandered over to the stack of albums. There was a distinct pleasure in discovering that his collection contained much of the same music she had in her own. She tried to subdue her reaction. It meant nothing, she told herself, selecting something rich and elegant from the eighteenth century.

"Music to ravish the senses," Wade said, walking into the living room with two steaming mugs a few moments later. He surveyed her as she sat curled in the corner of the leather couch. "And a woman who does the same."

Elissa felt her body react to the expression in his eyes. Knowing oneself desired was a seductive thing, she realized dimly as he set the mugs on the coffee table and walked over to the hearth. She watched, sipping at the steaming, soothing brew, as he dropped to one knee and expertly lit the fire. Wade Taggert seemed expert at everything he did.

"Have you ever," she whispered slowly as he straightened and moved back to the couch, "gotten into a situation you couldn't handle?"

He sank heavily down beside her, reaching for his own mug. For a second he seemed preoccupied with the toddy, and then his mouth quirked fractionally.

"I've learned one can handle almost anything if one is persistent enough."

"You mean, reach out and grab the matter by the throat and hang on until everyone else gives up?" Elissa felt her own lips shape into a smile.

"Something like that." He grinned, setting his mug back down on the table and taking hers out of her hands to do the same.

"And would you," she breathed as he pulled her into his arms with an overwhelming, thrilling strength, "be as persistent in a situation where you knew you'd made a mistake? That you'd been wrong or had misjudged completely?"

His mouth hovered a bare inch over hers as he cradled her in his arms across his lap. "Being right or wrong," he grated roughly, "doesn't particularly affect a man's desire." He settled a very tiny little kiss at the extreme edge of her lips. Then he tried another and another. . . .

"I thought we were going to talk," she managed between the enthralling, tempting little kisses. She felt his hand stroke the length of her body in a slow, languid, exploring caress that made her feel warm and wanted.

"We are. But I think we'll do it later. Right now all I can concentrate on is how good you feel in my arms."

Elissa struggled to maintain a hold on her plans for Sunday evening. But it was becoming clear that she had made a serious mistake allowing Wade to bring her home tonight. The tiny kisses being rained on her mouth were rapidly becoming insufficient to satisfy the desire they aroused. She wanted more. More of the tiny kisses, more of Wade's strength.

"You are so soft, so vibrant," he said against the skin of her throat, his voice husky with desire. "I love to feel you come alive when I'm holding you."

Elissa stirred under his hand, his words entering her head but not making the sense they should have made. His voice was like the music in the background; only another element in the seduction. And there were so many elements it was impossible to isolate and pay attention to any particular one!

How was she going to stop him this evening? she wondered, drawing in her breath as his fingers slid down the zipper of her dress. She had to find a way, of course. Everything tomorrow night depended on her not letting tonight get out of control.

His fingers traced delicate, fluttering patterns along her back and shoulders as the bodice of the dress was lowered. She would only let this go on a few minutes longer, Elissa promised herself, lifting her hands to find the black hair behind his ears. Enroute she used her nails gently, provocatively, on the tips of his earlobes and felt him shudder in response. Instantly the tiny butterfly kisses on her mouth began to deepen.

Elissa's fingertips clenched spasmodically as she felt her lips forced gently, inevitably, apart, and her lashes fluttered tightly closed as his tongue pressed the intimacy far into the territory of her mouth. She felt him loosen the clasp of her bra and she shivered, waiting with a sensual expectancy for the touch of his hand on her breast.

But it didn't come. Instead his warm, strong fingers slid between her breasts, down to rest for a moment on the small curve of her stomach and then move around her waist to the sensitive base of her spine. She moaned in the back of her throat and twisted against the crisp whiteness of his shirt.

"Elissa . . ." he breathed thickly, with growing, devouring urgency. "My sweet. I've waited too long to make you mine . . ."

Again the words floated into her head, and again she made a halfhearted attempt to comprehend the seriousness of the situation. She must get back to her own apartment, she knew. It was very important. And she would. Shortly.

But first . . . Her fingers undid the buttons of his shirt, and Elissa heard him groan, a thread of sound from deep inside him that sounded like a strange, masculine cross between laughter and impatient desire as she fumbled with the knot of his tie. But in a moment she had it free, and her nails raked lovingly across his skin, seeking the lines of his ribs and the curling hairs of his chest.

His hand was on her leg now, stroking, massaging, teasing the curve of her calf and the area behind her knee. Gently, insistently, he began to separate her legs, searching for the softness of her inner thigh. The hem of the dress was gliding higher, and soon she would be completely exposed to the hungry, flaming gray depths of his eyes.

And Elissa, as she had known deep in her heart tonight, realized that she wasn't going to demand to be taken back to her apartment. This was where she wanted to be. Always. She sighed with surrender and something more. Something that wanted to give more than her body to Wade. Something that wanted to give her heart and soul . . .

It was not common sense or belated memory of her unfulfilled revenge which brought Elissa back to reality with a shattering violence. It was an altogether mundane, chance occurrence.

The doorbell rang. And kept on ringing. It rang until Wade finally surfaced sufficiently to realize he had company.

Chapter 11

"Damn!" Wade's single, fiercely muttered epithet cut through the remainder of Elissa's fog.

"Someone at the door," she murmured unnecessarily as he helped her to a sitting position and quickly zipped up her dress. She watched him warily, not needing to be told that this was her escape. She would never have been able to make it on her own. With a rush of self-disgust she acknowledged that fact.

"I know," he growled. "I'll get rid of whoever it is and be right back, honey. Stay right where you are," he added, his eyes smiling down at her with heated promise. He put his hand for an instant over her breast in a mark of possession that remained as he got to his feet and stalked to the door.

Elissa twisted around on the couch to watch as he flung open the door with an annoyed, brusque motion. She would have to be ready to act when he had dismissed the caller, she told herself violently, her hands thrusting through her auburn hair. She wouldn't be able to risk any more of his caresses tonight. That way lay open disaster.

"Terry! What the hell are you doing here?"

Elissa jumped at the astonished note in Wade's voice. She couldn't see who stood on the other side of the door, but she could hear the throaty feminine greeting.

"I came to see you, darling. What else would I be doing here? My plane landed about an hour ago and I finally got a cab . . ."

Elissa watched, her heart in her throat, as a blond, beautiful, and expensively dressed woman floated gracefully across the threshold. Not just any sort of blond, Elissa thought grimly, her right hand curling unconsciously into a fist. But the stunning, artfully colored-to-imitate-the-sun blond that only California could produce. The woman was tall, model tall. But her figure was more voluptuous than any model's, and she wore her deceptively casual red silk blouse unbuttoned far enough to make sure that much was obvious. Sleek-fitting jeans worn with high heels completed the West Coast look. The gold chains around the slender neck and woven through the belt loops of the jeans were the finishing touch. Elissa decided she hated the woman on sight.

"I tried calling from the airport," the woman went on, handing Wade her fur jacket and lifting her hands to fluff the ends of her shoulder-length wind-blown hair. "But when there was no answer I decided to grab a cab and take a chance on finding you at home by the time I got here."

"We only arrived home a short time ago," Wade drawled meaningfully, his eyes going toward Elissa, who sat tightly coiled on the couch, her clenched hand out of sight behind the leather cushion.

"Oh, you have company!" Terry exclaimed, not sounding the least upset as she swung around to follow Wade's gaze. Something cool and calculating flashed briefly in the vividly made-up blue eyes which clashed with Elissa's, and then the mysterious Terry smiled. She was, perhaps, twenty-two or twenty-three.

"Terry," Wade began firmly, "I'd like you to meet Elissa Sheldon. My fiancée. Elissa, this is Terry Roberts . . ."

"Fiancée!" Terry turned her head to fling a laughing, disbelieving smile over her shoulder at Wade, who acknowledged it with a repressively lifted eyebrow.

"Fiancée," he repeated flatly, inviting no further comments from his guest.

"Terry Roberts," Elissa mused, striving to

find a way of holding her own in this triangle. "Any relation to John R.?"

"Oh, yes," Terry nodded agreeably, moving leisurely over to stand beside the fire, her hands clasped behind her back, her mouth turned upward in sultry challenge. "The boss's daughter."

The daughter of the head of CompuDesign, Elissa thought, absorbing the implications as she forced an automatic smile. Here to see her good friend Wade Taggert, who was being groomed to take over Daddy's position.

"Fascinating. You've come a long way this evening. How fortunate for you Wade was home." Elissa decided she could drawl her words just as challengingly as Terry Roberts could.

"Isn't it, though," Terry murmured brightly, flicking a glance across the room at Wade, who was moving slowly toward Elissa. If she hadn't known better, Elissa thought suddenly, she would have interpreted his action as almost protective, as if he would put himself between her and Terry. "I would have had to take a cab back to the airport and find a motel . . ." Terry let the words taper off, making it obvious that she now expected to spend the night at Wade's.

"Where's your luggage, Terry?" Wade's

voice had the edge of the whip in it, and Elissa could sense his irritation as if it were a physical presence.

"The cabdriver left it on the steps out front," the blond pouted vaguely, her inquisitive blue eyes going back to Elissa's cool expression.

"Fine. I'll put it in the Jag," Wade declared forcefully, heading back toward the door.

Terry frowned ever so slightly. "Why put it in the car?"

"Why do you think?" he shot back before disappearing out the door. "So that you'll have it when I take you to the motel!"

For an instant after he left silence reigned in the room, only the crackling of the fire daring to break it. Terry's blue eyes held a contemptuous gleam that made Elissa decide this was one young woman she wasn't going to go out of her way to charm. She would much prefer to strangle her!

"Fiancée. How interesting." Terry smiled chillingly. "How long have you been engaged to Wade, Elissa?"

"The engagement party is tomorrow evening."

"A very new arrangement, then?" Terry's smile dropped another couple of degrees.

"Very."

"I must congratulate you. You've worked rather quickly," Terry commended icily. "How long have you known Wade was in line for my father's position?"

"Since almost the first day he took over the Seattle office." Elissa smiled politely.

Terry began to amble around the room in a slinky, knowing fashion, pretending to examine the furniture, the books on the shelves, and other aspects of Wade's home. Elissa watched her as if she were watching a snake.

"Well, I can't fault your choice, Elissa," Terry murmured idly. "Although, personally, I wouldn't want any male who was on the rebound. . . ." She glanced over her shoulder to see how this news settled. Elissa merely stared back at her.

"I turned him down two months ago, you see," Terry announced smoothly.

"Did you?" Elissa felt her old instincts regarding other people awaken. It was so easy to know what others wanted, she thought. So easy to know what they were thinking, how their minds worked. So easy to know when they lied. . . .

Terry nodded, and Elissa could almost hear the plotting going on in the other woman's mind. "We had a fight," she began, pausing in front of one of the stark paintings and frowning at it. "He can be very possessive, you know," she added with a little disparaging gesture of her red-nailed fingers. "I lost my temper, and the next thing I knew he'd accepted this position in Seattle. I thought I'd give him time to miss me and then tell him all was forgiven . . ."

"What do you think of the painting, Terry?" Elissa whispered carefully, every sense alert.

"This thing?" Terry grimaced, nodding at the seascape. "I told him before he left California he should get rid of it. It doesn't do a thing for the rest of the furniture. I can't understand why he bought it in the first place!"

"Can't you?" Elissa breathed questioningly.

"I suppose he liked the artist personally and wanted to do him a favor or something," Terry said offhandedly. "I don't care. Whatever the reason, it's going to be gone as soon as I move in."

Elissa could have laughed if she weren't so close to tears. Terry didn't even know! Didn't she realize how much Wade was in that painting? What a little blond-brained fool! Whatever category Terry Roberts had occupied in Wade's life, it definitely hadn't been the long-lasting one!

"But you won't be moving in, Terry." Wade's voice came from where he stood lounging in the doorway behind the two women. "Not now, not ever. You've known from the beginning that you're nothing more to me than the daughter of the man for whom I work. And this little business of showing up on my doorstep in the middle of the night wouldn't have impressed John R. in the least." He walked into the room, shutting the door behind him.

Elissa shivered at the grim set of his face as he came forward to confront the sulky-mouthed blond. Didn't Terry have the sense to see she'd annoyed Wade Taggert?

"He knows me too well, Terry," Wade went on calmly. "He would never buy the scene you're trying to arrange. He'd never believe I'd seduce you."

"Why not?" Terry demanded, a wave of spite clouding her throaty voice as the pout turned into a full-fledged glare. She suddenly appeared very, very young.

"Two reasons," Wade drawled. "One, by the time you get back home tomorrow night the news of my engagement will already have reached him; and two . . ."

Terry lifted her head challengingly, apparently not seeing anything she couldn't overcome in the first reason.

"And two," Wade repeated devastatingly, "he knows I want his job too damn much to risk messing around with his daughter!"

Elissa winced at the bluntness of his words. She couldn't blame the other woman for looking as if she were on the verge of tears. What female wants to be told a job is more important than she is? But even as the thought went through her mind, she realized Wade had invented reason number two on the spur of the moment. If he'd wanted Terry Roberts, he would have taken her. Wade took whatever he wanted in life. Hadn't he told her that this evening? And if he'd wanted Terry *and* her father's job, he would have gotten both. He'd simply have fought until everyone else surrendered.

But Terry bought reason number two, hook, line, and sinker. It made perfect sense to her, Elissa saw as she watched the little drama. Just as Terry had never realized in the time she'd known Wade that the paintings on his walls held a part of him, so she lacked any real understanding of the man's nature. She didn't know a real wolf when she saw one.

"Let's go, Terry," Wade growled. "In the car. Elissa, you can wait —"

"I'm coming with you," Elissa declared, rising unsteadily but determinedly to her feet. This was her one chance tonight, and she had to take it. There would be no hope at all for her if she sat meekly waiting for Wade to return and claim his bride-to-be. No hope at all for revenge. . . .

"That's not necessary," Wade began, frowning heavily as he met her eyes across the room.

"Oh, but it is," she corrected gamely, essaying a smile. Her blue-green eyes glittered with her determination. "After all, we have a big day ahead of us tomorrow preparing for the party, don't we? I need some sleep, Wade. You can take me home." She started toward the door, ignoring the scowling blond and the rising thunder in Wade's eyes. Head high, she walked to the door and waited with a supreme assurance she was far from feeling for the other two to follow.

"Wade, this is ridiculous," Terry began. "There's no reason I can't stay here tonight —"

"Shut up, Terry."

Elissa could feel Wade's eyes on her as she led the way out into the cold night toward the car. But he said nothing, stuffing both women into the Jaguar with a complete lack of chivalry and sliding into the driver's seat to twist the key viciously in the ignition. He was furious, Elissa thought, and decided to take a few precautions.

"You can let me off first," she informed him coolly, not daring to glance at his stern profile.

"The hell I will," he retorted, slamming the car into gear.

"Please, Wade?" she tried, deliberately injecting into her tone, the soft pleading that she had discovered the night he had threatened to beat her. "I'm exhausted. It's been a frantic week, and I want to be halfway fresh for tomorrow evening. Everyone will be there . . ."

"Elissa, I want to talk to you," he began firmly. Both of them ignored Terry, who sat in the back seat and took in every word. Elissa could feel her lapping up the budding argument and hated the idea of the other woman's witnessing the scene. But there was no help for it. She had to get safely back to her apartment.

"Wade, we'll have all the time in the world to talk tomorrow after the party." Elissa put out a gentle hand to touch his sleeve, begging for his understanding. "I want to go home."

He was silent a moment, as if turning her words and her pleading over and over in his mind, and then she sensed his hesitation and knew she had won.

"All right, Elissa," he finally agreed, sounding resigned but not satisfied. "I'll take you home."

Elissa could feel Terry's air of excited triumph, but it didn't affect her at all. Wade would take Terry to a motel and leave her there. Elissa was as certain of that as she had ever been about anything in her life. Terry represented no danger and she never would. The danger between Elissa and Wade went deeper and held much more risk than a spoiled, flighty young woman's attempts to snag herself a husband.

Wade let Elissa go at the elevators in the lobby of the apartment building, his eyes reflecting his dissatisfaction with events but also his reluctant agreement to abide by her wishes.

"I have a feeling this is a mistake." He sighed ruefully, pulling her roughly into his arms. "Damn that little bubblehead! If it weren't for her . . ."

Elissa summoned a small teasing grin. "Are there a lot more like her trailing you around the countryside?"

"No, thank God! I'm going to wire her father in the morning and advise a severe . . ."

"Beating?" Elissa suggested demurely.

"A severe cutback in her allowance," Wade concluded smoothly. "Money is the surest way of controlling a spoiled little brat like Terry Roberts."

"But not me?" Elissa taunted lightly, grateful that he wasn't going to protest her decision to return to the apartment.

"No, not you," he murmured richly, lowering his head to kiss her quickly, almost harshly. "You require more subtle methods."

She had told Wade she needed sleep, Elissa thought several hours later as she lay awake in her bed and watched shadows on the ceiling. But sleep was a long time coming tonight. With a restless movement Elissa turned on her side, pounding the hapless pillow in an attempt to fluff it. This was the second sleepless night since she'd gotten involved with one Wade Taggert, she reminded herself grimly. But soon the man and all his arrogant, demanding ways would be behind her. Tomorrow night, she vowed for the thousandth time, she would put a fine and mighty end to the war game they had been playing.

Once more she tried to formulate the exact manner in which she would announce to Wade that she had no intention of marrying him and that he could take his ring and his job and go jump in Lake Washington. And once again it proved incredibly difficult to work through the scene in her mind. Every time she tried, memories of his paintings or the way he talked to her or the way he kissed her kept interfering.

But he didn't love her, she thought furiously. A man who loved her would never have accused her of the things Wade Taggert had accused her of. He would never have believed the worst of her. Damn it, no one ever believed the worst of her!

But, then, Wade had never claimed to love her, had he? Only to desire her.

But such desire, she thought, catching her breath in the darkness. It was outside her experience. Did it spring from the loneliness, the independence, and the power she saw in his paintings? Did he really believe she could assuage it for him?

No, she mustn't think along those lines. She had her own role to play in the last act of the charade, and it did not include falling in love with her tormentor.

Falling in love! Elissa could have wept then. And, like sleepless nights, weeping was alien to her. Life was much too comfortable and contented to make crying into her pillow necessary. And she could not, must not, love a man who thought so little of her! He had deserved being tricked into making the proposal, and he was going to deserve having her walk out the door laughing, the proposal thrown back at him. In front of all his employees!

Desperately Elissa forced herself to consider that. It would be the ultimate humiliation if she handed him her resignation from CompuDesign and the ring in front of the entire staff.

It was an outrageous, horrifying thought, and it made Elissa sit straight up in bed. Would she have the nerve? Could she possibly cause a scene of that magnitude? Upset the entire staff? It was so utterly unlike her to even consider doing such a thing — regardless of the provocation!

But the past week had made Elissa uncomfortably aware of aspects of her nature she hadn't faced before. She had discovered a temper which could plot revenge on an undreamed-of scale. She had discovered a level of passion within herself she hadn't thought any man could arouse. She had been confronted with the notion that she might have been guilty of using her innate ability to charm for her own ends. She had found an element of excitement in life she hadn't ever expected to encounter in the real world. An excitement she had thought reserved for her flights of imagination in her paintings. And, above all, she had met a man who understood all of those things. He understood everything except the fact that she would never in a million years have tried to sleep her way up the ladder of success.

Elissa muttered a low, tense oath that would have done justice to a cowboy's and threw back the covers. She padded across the room and turned the painting which rested against the wall around so that the moonlight fell on it.

She had gone ahead and finished the small canvas because she had never intended to obey Wade's injunction to give it to him for a wedding gift. It didn't matter what she put into the painting, because he would never see the result.

But she would see it, Elissa thought sadly, despairingly. Even if she destroyed it, she would see it in her mind's eye for the rest of her life. Hopelessly she turned the acrylic creation back to the wall, knowing that what it revealed was something she would have to learn to live with. A legacy from the one period of disturbance and discomfort in an otherwise smooth and comfortable life.

But she was committed to her revenge, Elissa told herself grimly, walking over to the window and gazing unseeingly out at the city lights. What option did she have? She couldn't possibly marry a man who didn't love her and who had, from the beginning, thought her capable of a complete lack of scruples.

But what if he genuinely needed her? a small voice asked beguilingly. What if he truly wanted and needed her? Had pursued her because she was important to him even though he thought her capable of such awful things?

Elissa shook her head in self-anger. Who was she kidding? She was seeking an excuse, a reason for marrying a man she should despise. Why this powerful inner pull to reach out and accept what he offered? And how could she do that in good conscience? She had tricked him into offering marriage. She didn't want his ring, knowing it had not been freely given, that he had only upped the ante in order to stay in the game. . . .

Elissa fumbled her way back to bed. It was all so horribly confusing, and time was running out so quickly. . . .

None of the doubts or confusion disappeared in the night. Morning brought only a continuation of the endless debate going on in Elissa's head, a debate she thought might be affecting her very sanity. She spent the day listlessly doing housework in some ill-defined attempt to work out the frustration and fear. But it had little effect.

Time ticked inevitably past, and all too soon she had to begin preparing for her grand evening scene.

The least she could do, Elissa decided with defiance and determination, was dress for the event. She pulled the glittering blue-green sheath out of the closet with a vicious gesture that nearly tore it. The action made her realize the state of her nerves, and she took several deep breaths before proceeding to dress.

The severely cut dress, bought a few months ago for a party which Elissa had changed her mind about attending, slithered down over her head, settling with well-cut precision around her slender curves. The long sleeves were close-fitting, and the plain deeply rounded collar set off the line of neck and throat to perfection. The color was an ideal foil for the dark red of her hair and it matched her eyes.

This was a night when she would need all the witchcraft Wade had accused her of having, Elissa decided, reaching into the closet for a pair of evening slippers that were little more than sandals on heels. She dug through her small collection of jewelry for the tiny gold earrings she liked and a discreet gold necklace. The hunt for the proper jewelry made her think of the ring Wade would be giving her tonight, and she grimaced in dismay.

A glance at the clock while she was brushing the shining mass of her hair drove home the information that time had indeed evaporated. It was four o'clock, and she had promised Wade she would be at his house by four-thirty. He had wanted to pick her up, she but had assured him that was a waste.

She didn't want to think about the real reason she needed her own car tonight.

At precisely four-thirty, Elissa stood on the steps of Wade's town house and prepared for the worst evening of her life. It took all her courage just to lift her hand to knock.

Almost as soon as she had done so, the door was pulled open and Wade was drinking in the sight of her. Almost literally drinking it in, Elissa thought dimly. The hunger and thirst in his eyes were living things that reached out to lap at her body and soul, threatening to take them both in one swallow.

"Elissa," he breathed, putting out a hand to encircle her neck and pull her over the threshold into his arms. "I thought you'd never get here!" He pinned her against him and bent to kiss the curve of her shoulder revealed by the round neck of the dress. His lips seemed to burn for a moment, and then he was gazing down into her eyes again.

"It's . . . it's just four-thirty. I'm on time," she protested tremulously. How was she going to do it? How was she going to exact her revenge? Now? Before the others arrived? Later, when it would be far more humiliating and dramatic? Elissa felt the panic begin to rise.

"How can you say you're on time when you should have been here this morning, waking up in my bed?" he demanded with a rough, uncertain humor that touched her.

"Speaking of which," she tried to say pertly, stepping aside so he could close the door behind her, "did you manage to get your dear acquaintance on a plane bound for California?"

"Beats me." Wade grinned, taking her hand and pulling her toward the kitchen, where bottles and quantities of food filled the counters. "I stuck her in a motel by the airport last night, sent a wire off to John R. telling him where she was, and forgot about it."

"Roberts won't, uh, believe you might truly have compromised her?" Elissa asked dryly, staring at all the beautifully prepared trays of food.

"In my wire I made a point of mentioning

my engagement," Wade admitted, stacking glasses. "But even without that he would have had the sense to know whether to believe me or his daughter. He loves her, but he's not blind to her faults."

"Fathers have been known to lose some of their rational view of life when presented with a situation involving a daughter."

"Or a wife?" he suggested, pausing in his task to trap her gaze with his own. "Are you saying men aren't always rational about women in general?"

Elissa swallowed and tried to smile.

"You could be right, you know," Wade went on easily, pushing a pile of napkins into her hand. She remembered having done something similar to him when he'd appeared at her party the week before. The memory made her face burn. "That's why I sent the telegram and mentioned my charming fiancée. Better to be safe than sorry."

"And you do want his job," she shot back banteringly.

"Not badly enough to marry his daughter," Wade declared fervently. "You can put those napkins on the table in the corner. I thought we'd scatter the food trays around the room."

"Did you do all this?" she asked in amazement, indicating all the trays.

"Now, what do you think? Do I look like every woman's dream of a man who's good in the kitchen? I ordered everything from caterer's. The stuff arrived a couple of hours ago." He chuckled, picking up one of the trays.

"You may not be an old hand in the kitchen, but you seem to know the easiest way to manage a cocktail party," Elissa commented, following him obediently around the living room with her piles of napkins.

"I've done a certain amount of entertaining. To an extent, it's almost a necessity in business." He shrugged. "When I have you to act as hostess, however, my reputation as a giver of good parties should skyrocket!"

Elissa felt her palms moisten as five o'clock approached. Perhaps she should simply get it over with now before anyone arrived. She tried to imagine telling Wade just then that she wasn't going through with the marriage and that he could have her damn job, too. A realistic picture failed to materialize in her mind.

By the time the first guests began arriving, Elissa was a nervous wreck. It was all she could do to maintain a semblance of normality, although no one seemed to notice her discomfort as they came through the door. They were all too concerned about being at a party given by the boss, she thought after a moment. His invitation to the staff had, after all, been tantamount to a command. It was no wonder virtually everyone was showing up — and on time! Elissa began to experience a touch of hysteria. No one but Marie knew the reason for the party yet. His announcement was going to be a surprise, Wade had told her.

Some familiar instinct took over as Elissa automatically began chatting with new arrivals, putting them at ease. It gave her a chance to recover her failing nerve as the soothing patter covered the lack of enthusiasm she knew she would be projecting if anyone cared to look beneath the surface.

But no one ever looked that deep except Wade, and he made no mention of Elissa's unease. Perhaps he hadn't notice it. He had his hands full, pouring drinks and playing host. A difficult role for a wolf, Elissa thought, torn between laughter and despair. The man would be much better off with a wife to help him through the difficulties of business socializing.

And all she had to do was keep her mouth shut and she could be that wife. No, Elissa thought again and again. She would not marry a man who thought her so unprincipled!

Then what was she going to do? She would have to act soon. It was going on six o'clock, and Wade would surely make his announcement at any moment while the crowd was at its peak. . . .

Even as the thought came into her head she saw Wade catch her eye from the other side of the room and grin. The look on his face stopped her in her tracks. He was going to do it now. She knew it. God help her, what was she going to do about it? This was the moment. The moment all her plans had been aiming toward. Across the room Marie smiled knowingly.

Heart pounding, Elissa watched Wade cheerfully call for everyone's attention. He got it immediately, naturally; he was the boss.

"There is an ulterior motive for the party this evening," Wade began as soon as the room had fallen silent. Very carefully Elissa began edging her way toward him. She had never been so torn or terrified in her life. She had to act. She had to!

Her mind whirling, she listened to him explain the reason for the occasion and heard the combined gasp of amazement from the crowd as he told them he was announcing his engagement to Elissa Sheldon.

And then the cries of congratulations and

surprise were pouring over her as she was helped along her way to stand beside Wade.

"No wonder she didn't get the promotion!" she heard someone mutter speculatively nearby. "It would have looked pretty bad for Wade to promote her one week and get engaged to her the next. People would have talked . . ."

"Not about Elissa," another voice chimed in with great certainty.

"No, not about Elissa," the first speaker agreed. "But Wade might have thought they would. After all, he doesn't know her like we do . . ."

The words were a kind of balm to Elissa's ears, and she wondered if Wade had heard them. She doubted it. Even if he had, he would only have laughed.

She went forward more steadily now, accepting the hand held out to her and letting him pull her close to his side. He was smiling, warmly, intimately, hungrily, down into her eyes, and she was abruptly aware that he had the ring box in his other hand.

"My sweet witch," he whispered under cover of the laughter and cheers as he slipped the ring on her finger. And then he kissed her lightly, gently.

In that moment the one unwavering fact which stuck out in Elissa's thoughts wasn't that her moment of revenge had arrived. It was that she had tricked him into doing this. Tricked him into marriage when he had only wanted to toy with her for a time. When all he desired was a woman who could appease the loneliness of a wolf. A woman who could put some softness into a life of near-constant battle.

Elissa hesitated and was lost. When she opened her eyes as he lifted his mouth from hers, the first thing she saw was the seascape on the wall behind him, and she finally admitted the truth. She loved him. She loved this man who had turned her comfortable world upside down and seen aspects of her no one else knew existed. She loved a man she had tricked into marriage.

For Elissa the rest of the evening went by in a whirl of incomprehensible sounds, conversations, and laughter. A laughter which she could not share in her heart. This was her engagement party, and she had never been more miserable in her life.

The party lasted much too long. It was supposed to be over by seven, but the last of the guests hung around until eight. Even as she watched them out the door, Elissa realized she would rather they stayed. Anything to postpone the coming confrontation with her fiancé. For sometime during the course of the evening it had become painfully clear to Elissa what needed to be said. She could not humiliate the man she loved by throwing his proposal back in his face in front of his guests, and she could not marry a man she had deceived in making that proposal in the first place.

"I thought," Wade murmured softly, turning to rake her with his hungry glance as he closed the door on the last of his guests, "that I'd never get you to myself! Come here and let me nibble on you for a while!"

Elissa stood perfectly still, her hands clasped in front of her, and forced herself to say the words which must be said.

"Wade, I must talk to you."

He loosened his tie and opened the collar of his shirt, his gaze never leaving her tense face. The blue-green gems of her eyes seemed huge and strangely lit, holding his full attention.

"We'll talk, Elissa," he promised in a slow, thrilling tone that sent shivers through her. "I know there are things which must be clear between us. But not yet. Not until I've made you mine." He started forward slowly. "Can you understand that, honey? Can you understand how it is for a man who must know his woman accepts his claim? Come close, Elissa, and let me hold you. Let me show you what I've been aching to show you since the day I first saw you. . . ."

"You can't put me off tonight, Wade." She smiled sadly. "You must listen to me, and then . . ."

"Then what, Elissa?" he prompted, halting a few feet away and watching her intently.

"Then you can do as you want."

"Take what I want?"

She drew a gulping breath. "Yes."

"All right, tell me what it is that's put the fear in your eyes tonight, little witch. Yes, I've seen it," he went on heavily. "Did you think you could hide such a thing from me? But I have the cure for it, sweetheart . . ."

"Wade! Will you stop trying to seduce me and listen to what I have to say?" She almost screamed the words at him, and then she flushed, alarmed at her lack of control. "I tricked you into this, Wade! Don't you realize that? I planned it all along. I wanted you to pay for what you'd done by denying me that promotion because you thought I was sleeping with Martin Randolph!"

She drew a deep breath and plunged on. Once stated, the words wouldn't be halted. "I got lucky, or so I thought, when it turned out you wanted me enough to meet the offer you thought I was getting from Dean

Norwood. I lied about that. He never offered to marry me. Do you realize what I'm saying? I tricked you. I had plans for tonight, plans you never knew about. I was going to wait until the moment you put the ring on my finger, and then I was going to take it off and fling at your feet and tell you to go to hell along with the stupid job possibilities you were holding out as a lure!"

Elissa paused for another gulp of air. "It was going to be a grand, thoroughly humiliating scene, you understand. One that would tear a wide strip out of your ego and teach you a lesson about jumping to conclusions. And the whole thing blew up in my face when I realized I loved you."

She turned away to stare into the fire he had built earlier, supremely conscious of his massive presence behind her but unable to meet the glittering look which had sprung alive in his eyes.

"I'll go with you to Victoria, Wade, if that's what you want. But I'll go as your woman, not your wife. I couldn't bear to have you marry me because that was the only way you thought you could get me," she breathed in a hushed voice. There. She had done all she could to repair the damage she had wrought. It was in Wade's hands now. Whatever he decided would be binding. At least she would have the miserable satisfaction of knowing she had been completely honest at last.

"And just who," he grated in measured, heart-jolting tones behind her, "do you think was tricking whom?"

Chapter 12

"You've been outclassed, outmaneuvered, and out-tricked every step of the way, my lovely. Ever since I walked into that damn party of yours and was forced to realize I'd made the biggest mistake of my life!"

Elissa whirled, reacting as much to the raw, rasping pain in his voice as to the words themselves. "Wade! What are you saying?" she gasped, lifting wide, uncomprehending eyes to meet the unfathomable gray depths of his gaze. Her heart had begun to pound with an incredulous hope.

"I think," Wade went on judiciously, jamming his hands into his pockets and facing her, feet slightly spread as if he would brace himself, "that I knew before I arrived at the party that I'd made a hell of a miscalculation. I think I knew it the moment I hit you with my accusation that Friday afternoon when I told you I wasn't giving you the job. But I had been so blinded by sheer, raving jealousy when I'd seen you meet Randolph after work that all I could think of was that you must be seeing him on the sly. I put myself in Randolph's place, you see," Wade went on with a wry twist of his hard mouth. "I knew if I managed to get you to meet me after work there wouldn't be a damned platonic thing about it!"

"Wade!" Elissa's sea-colored eyes began to glow. She took a small step toward him but stopped when he lifted a hand to ward her off.

"No, honey, you'd better hear it all first. You started it!" He seemed to gather himself for his next words. "So, where was I? Oh, yes. Standing in your doorway staring into a room full of people there to celebrate June Randolph's birthday. Exactly as you had claimed. I had been a first-class jealous fool and I'd blown everything. There was nothing for it but to keep going. I couldn't think of anything else to do. I spent the whole time at the party trying to figure a way to recover to another, more flexible position, and I couldn't think of one. If I backed down and admitted I'd made a mistake, you'd laugh in my face and probably never speak to me again."

Wade shook his head, running his fingers through his hair in a gesture of male disgust. "On the other hand, I was learning a lot about you in a hurry. I saw those paintings on your wall, saw the books in your bedroom, and, most of all, I saw the satisfaction in your eyes when you thought you'd won. It occurred to me that the best, perhaps the only way to keep you on my hook was to make you think victory wasn't going to be all that easy."

"And everything had always been so easy for me?" Elissa smiled, laughter warming her eyes.

"Something like that," he admitted ruefully, slanting her a quick, wry glance. "I could see the lack of challenge in your life, but I could also see the willingness to take on a challenge in your eyes and in your paintings. I decided to give you a toy to play with long enough to whet your appetite."

"A witch's toy?" she whispered happily.

"Yes."

"Oh, Wade," she breathed joyously. Still neither of them moved. "Why didn't you tell me?"

"I was going to try to explain everything last night. I kept asking if you wanted to talk about our future, if you'll recall, but you kept shying away from it. I wasn't sure what to do, but I decided the most straightforward approach was probably the best under the circumstances. . . ."

"So you were going to bring me back here

and make love to me and then confess all?" she demanded, laughter bubbling up inside.

"In that order," he admitted. "When that didn't pan out, I decided to try it again tonight. It was becoming increasingly important to make love to you, lady witch," he growled. "I had tried to avoid it while I was securing you in the net."

"Why?"

"Because I knew that once I had you would realize the full extent of your power over me. I needed to keep you tantalized, curious, off balance, and, perhaps, looking for revenge . . ."

"You knew? You knew I was plotting terrible things?"

"I knew I'd aroused your temper as well as your interest." He smiled bleakly. "It seemed likely you'd go looking for a bit of your own back if there was a way to get it. But I also knew you were coming to know me better, and I started banking on the fact that you were basically too gentle, too warmhearted, to send me back to my paintings where I belong. You thought I'd made things easy for your plans of revenge when I agreed to marry you, but the truth is, as far as I was concerned, you fell into my palm like a ripe plum!"

"But I tricked you that night you came

back from California! I deliberately brought up the subject of Dean Norwood!"

"As I said, I got lucky. All I was aiming for was to get you to stop seeing him. I figured if I made love to you enough to make you realize I was a much more interesting proposition . . ."

"You never did intend to spend the night in my bed!" She remembered how he had refused to let her completely undress him.

"I didn't intend to, but I'm not sure I could have avoided it." He grinned, starting toward her finally and putting his hands on her shoulders. "But when marriage came into the matter I was suddenly aware of the fact that you had just given me several free moves ahead in our game. All I had to do was keep pushing along the lines you'd already started."

"Didn't you wonder why I was agreeing to the marriage?" Elissa whispered, standing quietly under his hands.

"I thought you probably had your own schemes going, but so long as they coincided with mine . . ." He left the sentence unfinished.

"You figured you'd just hang on until everyone else gave up?" she charged, laughing up at him with love.

"Yes!" The single word was ground out

with so much grim determination that Elissa believed him.

"What would you have done, Wade Taggert," she demanded boldly, "if I'd gone through with my own plans for this evening? If I'd really hurled the ring back in your face?"

"Beaten you in front of the entire assembled staff of CompuDesign," he retorted unhesitatingly.

Elissa tilted her head to one side and studied the innate arrogance and unshielded iron will in his face and shook her head. "You really mean that, don't you?"

His voice dropped to a new, thick, and almost unsteady pitch as he pulled her closer. "I love you. I couldn't have let you walk out of my life. Not when I was so close to . . ."

Elissa finished the sentence for him with a tiny, bantering grin. "Not when you were so close to winning?"

"I'm glad you understand me so well. It's going to make life much simpler in some ways," he muttered on a low groan of need. His hands slipped along her shoulders, sliding warmly up her throat to entwine themselves in her chair, and he lowered his head to take her lips.

"Do you really love me?" he asked on a thin thread of steel and anguish.

"Yes." Elissa saw the hunger in his eyes,

the wolf's hunger which was more than an appetite. It was a fundamental desire and need and wish and longing. And it was elaborately laced with love. Why hadn't she seen that from the beginning? "I love you, Wade, more than anything else on earth!"

"Or off it?" he charged just before his mouth touched hers.

"Or off it." She heard the deep sigh of pleasure, and then he was kissing her, a soft seal on their love. A binding, chaining, magical kiss that she would never forget. She felt the large hands in her hair tighten and instinctively moved closer to him.

And the doorbell sounded.

"Damn it to hell!" Wade muttered, not lifting his lips from hers. Elissa's eyes flew open, and she was looking directly into rueful gray pools of sheer masculine frustration. She wanted to laugh and knew the humor must be gleaming in her own gaze.

"Probably only a guest who forgot something," she whispered encouragingly.

"It must be that. I couldn't be so unlucky two nights in a row!" He groaned, reluctantly setting her back from him as the bell sounded yet again. An imperious, demanding, commanding summons that made Elissa lift a questioning eyebrow as Wade strode almost angrily to the door.

She saw the incredulous expression on Wade's face before she saw the man standing at the door.

"What the hell are you doing here?" Wade's voice held a new note which Elissa's interested ears picked up at once. The words were blunt enough, but they were tinged with respect.

"Am I too late for the party?" The stranger's voice was deep and gruff, and it suited him very well, Elissa decided as he stepped into the room. A big man, almost as big as Wade, he looked to be in his early sixties, and he also looked, she thought, like an older version of Wade. Not that the two men were similar physically. This man's hair was a rapidly thinning gray and the eyes were blue, not pools of ice and silver. No, the resemblance was more primitive and fundamental than a blood bond. There was the same air of ruthlessness, the same arrogance, the same independence. Another lone wolf. Elissa remembered where she'd seen eyes of that particular shade of blue.

Wade turned toward Elissa, and she could see the surprise still in his face.

"Elissa," he began very carefully, precisely, "may I present John R. Roberts, founder and head of CompuDesign? Our boss."

Elissa smiled straight into the blue eyes so like his daughter's and came forward with welcome and laughing grace. "I have always wondered," she remarked, lips curved dazzlingly, "what the *R* stood for!"

Twenty-four hours later Elissa sat in the middle of a huge four-poster bed which looked as if it had come from a seventeenth-century castle and waited for her husband to emerge from the bath. She fluffed the huge pillows and old-fashioned quilts which surrounded her and leaned back to study the canopy for a moment. She felt like a queen, she decided, her gaze moving on to enjoy the other antique furnishings. This could have easily been a room in a castle on another world for all the resemblance it bore to a modern bedroom. One could almost imagine a dragon standing guard at the gate and a strange moon outside the window. A good room in which to embark on an adventure. The crackle of a fire on the hearth was warming.

Elissa turned toward the sound of the opening bathroom door, her blue-green eyes full of dreams. Wade stood there, a towel wrapped carelessly around his lean waist, his dark hair damp from the shower. The leaping gray gaze raked possessively, lovingly, over the outline of his wife who had the sheet tucked up to her chin, and he grinned.

"You look right at home. A witch in her castle. They still had the sense to worry about witches in the seventeenth century, you know," he told her.

The firelight gleamed on his powerful, smoothly muscled body as he came toward her, turning off the lights behind him. But the flames on the hearth were no warmer than the ones in the silvery eyes. He stopped beside the high bed, watchful and clearly filled with anticipation.

"Did you bring my wedding present?" he demanded softly.

"Yes, Wade." She smiled, reaching for the small canvas she had propped beside the bed. "Did you remember mine?"

He said nothing, turning aside for a moment to pull a square, flat package from the luggage at the foot of the bed. Silently he handed it to her, accepting his present from her with an eagerness that touched her heart.

For a moment they both examined their gifts in the firelight. When they raised their eyes to meet each other's gaze, there was little need of speech. The paintings said it all.

Elissa looked again at the harsh, haunting outlines of the painting Wade had commissioned for her. The isolation and aloofness were still inherent qualities in the work, but there was a new element. There were figures in this painting. A woman sat high on a rock overlooking the sea, and her bare arm rested lovingly on the wolf at her side. She looked totally unafraid of the vicious creature beside her, and her red hair shone in the light of the sun. There was no reason for the woman to fear the beast, Elissa knew. The ruthlessness of the wolf was aimed at the outside world. The woman was well protected.

"I knew when I saw the beginnings of this the night I came to talk about the party arrangements that I couldn't lose in the end," Wade finally whispered deeply, glancing up again from his present. Elissa knew what he saw on the canvas in his hands. A fantasy castle standing on a peak in a scene from another planet. Unfamiliar twin moons threw unearthly light on a landscape full of strange beings and stranger flowers. On the parapet of the castle a woman waited for the black-and-silver wolf who was climbing the tumbling stairs to her side. The wolf looked as potentially lethal as the one in Wade's painting, but he carried a flower in his jaws.

"Well, witch" — Wade smiled with a thrilling, warning timber in his words as he placed the two paintings carefully beside the bed — "your wolf has waited long enough to know all of your magic." He pulled back the covers, letting the towel fall to the floor, and slid into the warm bed, reaching out to pull her close.

Elissa's eyes gleamed with love as she absorbed the unselfconscious male beauty of him. "Don't blame me for having to wait until tonight. *I* didn't have people dropping in at unexpected moments in my apartment!"

"Don't remind me!" He grimaced, his hand running over her modest, old-fashioned nightgown with its demure collar and ruffles and lace. "If it had been anyone besides John R. last night, I would have slammed the door in his face. I couldn't think of an excuse to send him to a motel!"

"I thought it was sweet of him to come all the way up from California to attend your engagement party and act as your best man."

"Honey, John R. Roberts is not a sweet man, I can guarantee you that much!" Wade grinned, his fingers toying lovingly with the ribbons at her throat. "He was there because he wanted to know what kind of woman had managed to charm his hand-picked heir apparent into marriage. He wanted to see if you were going to be an asset to the firm, nothing more!"

"Do you think I passed inspection?" She giggled, feeling the ribbons come undone beneath his hands.

"You charmed the socks off him, just like you do everyone else you decide to entrance and enchant, and you know it!"

"Would you still have married me even if John R. hadn't approved?" she whispered, feeling the heated touch of his fingers on her bare skin above the curve of her breast.

"I would have married you," he grated with sudden harsh intensity, his eyes darkening, "if all the dragons in the universe had stood in the way! My career, John R.'s approval, nothing in the world matters to me as much as you, my lady witch. I love you with the kind of love I didn't know existed until I set eyes on you. I would have done anything, fought anyone, played any game, in order to carry off my prize!"

Elissa's breath quickened at the fierceness in him, and she knew he meant every word. Then he lowered his lips to the hollow of her throat, and her lashes fluttered shut with the force of her clamoring emotions.

"I love you, Wade!"

"Not half as much as I love you, lady wife!" His voice was a husky, muffled growl against her skin as his lips followed the ever bolder path of his fingers.

Elissa reached out to first caress and then cling lovingly to the hard leanness of him, exulting in the strength beneath her questing hands. She moaned softly, luxuriously, as he slipped the nightgown off completely and leaned across to drop burning, stinging, entrancing kisses over every inch of her skin from throat to waist.

"Do you know how intoxicating it is," he grated roughly, hungrily, "to own full and exclusive rights to a genuine witch?" He raised himself to settle her more tightly against him, and the plundering, searching fingers of his hand wandered down below her waist, finding her intimate warmth.

Elissa shivered as she felt his nails grate roughly and then soothingly over her thighs, and her legs shifted languidly as her body arched instinctively. She heard his groan of desire and need as she sought the sensitive masculine nipples with her tongue and teeth and felt his rising passion.

His lips burned for a moment at her waist, and then he nipped the vulnerable flesh of her thigh, eliciting a tremor in her that seemed to increase his own passion by great bounds. His lovemaking grew increasingly demanding, inflamed.

"My God!" he breathed, "I don't think I can wait any longer for you, my little love. You pull me into your spells so quickly . . ."

"Love me, Wade," she gasped, clutching fiercely to him to draw him closer. "I need you so much!"

She felt him shift his weight, lowering himself onto her with urgency and power. Her legs were forced gently apart, making a place for him that he assumed with the authority and arrogance of a conqueror who loves the land he takes.

Elissa felt her body surrendering, enveloping, charming even as Wade claimed his witch with an uncompromising mastery. She gasped at the loving assault, wrapping her arms around his neck and holding him as close as it was possible for a man and a woman to be.

The rhythm and strength of Wade's lovemaking launched them into a glittering galaxy where Elissa viewed at first hand the stars and planets in her paintings. She cried out with the wonder of it and heard his wolfish growl of response. For an indefinable number of light-years they raced and soared through the universe and then, with shattering intensity, found themselves caught in the heart of an exploding sun. Slowly, slowly, they returned to earth, riding the last of the magic spell back into the witch's bedroom in the inn on the tip of Vancouver Island.

For a long time Wade simply held her close against him, his head buried in the pillow beside her as his body recuperated with long, full breaths. Elissa was content to curl into his heat and contemplate the wonder of being married to Wade Taggert. Eventually she felt him stir. The gray eyes opened and met hers.

"In the beginning," he told her finally, smilingly, "I thought I could handle your charms and spells, even when I found myself trapped in them. Now I realize I was only fooling myself. I may have caught you in my net, witch, but I'm in there with you. Promise me you'll never want to escape. I could never let you go!"

Elissa's full lips shaped into a warm, dazzling smile, her eyes full of reassurance and promise for the future. "You're not really a wolf, you know," she teased.

"No?" One black brow lifted interrogatingly.

"No. You're a sorcerer who uses the shape of a wolf because it suits your personality. But your spells are every bit as powerful as you claim mine are. And I am as thoroughly enmeshed in your magic net as it's possible for a woman to be. I would never leave, Wade. You make the magic and fantasy in my life real," she concluded simply.

"And to think," he murmured, his hand moving possessively across her bare skin, delighting in the texture of her, "that there was a time when I didn't believe in witches!"

There was a moment of contented, satisfied silence, and then the gray eyes began to gleam with a warning look Elissa recognized only too well.

"Wade?"

"Just thinking, honey."

"About what?" she prompted suspiciously.

"About what you said on the ferry coming over to Victoria. That business about quitting your job and going to work somewhere else because you can't abide working for a tyrant."

"Oh, that." She smiled serenely.

"That. I have some arguments to offer on the other side of the issue," he began purposefully, his fingers beginning to trace a more detailed pattern on her skin.

"You just want me to stay at CompuDesign so that you'll have me under your thumb all day long!"

He contrived to look hurt. "It's not that. It's only that I don't like the idea of you using your charms on some poor unsuspecting employer in order to land a fabulous new job."

"You're on a campaign to protect the employers of this world from the likes of me?" she enquired interestedly.

"My civic duty."

"Well, I'll listen to your arguments," she agreed generously. "But I can guarantee they won't change my mind."

"My arguments," he warned deeply, pulling her close, "aren't based on reason."

"No?"

"No," he assured her, lowering his mouth until he was a heartbeat away from her lips. The gleam in his eyes had erupted into flames. "They're based on magic, you see. Much more effective."

"For someone who once didn't believe in witches, you're learning fast." Elissa felt her pulse begin to throb and the excitement begin to build again.

"A wolf is a very practical creature. He uses whatever works. And against a witch the only weapon is magic."

And he proceeded to demonstrate.

About the Author

Stephanie James is a pseudonym for Jayne Ann Krentz, one of today's best-loved authors of women's fiction. With multiple *New York Times* bestselling novels to her credit, she is a prolific and innovative writer — much to the delight of her legions of fans around the world. She has delved into psychic elements, intrigue, fantasy, historical and even futuristic romances. Jayne lives in Seattle.

We hope you have enjoyed this Large Print book. Other Thorndike, Wheeler or Chivers Press Large Print books are available at your library or directly from the publishers.

For more information about current and upcoming titles, please call or write, without obligation, to:

Publisher
Thorndike Press
295 Kennedy Memorial Drive
Waterville, ME 04901
Tel. (800) 223-1244

Or visit our Web site at:
www.gale.com/thorndike
www.gale.com/wheeler

OR

Chivers Large Print
published by BBC Audiobooks Ltd
St James House, The Square
Lower Bristol Road
Bath BA2 3SB
England
Tel. +44(0) 800 136919
email: bbcaudiobooks@bbc.co.uk
www.bbcaudiobooks.co.uk

All our Large Print titles are designed for easy reading, and all our books are made to last.